CW01637605

by Malcolm Storer

When there is no desire, all things are at peace.

Lao Tzu, *Tao Te Ching.*

For Chikako

One

There it was. The house of their dreams: a detached Victorian red brick villa set in ten acres of Cheshire countryside.

"Oh my God!" exclaimed Paul. "It's perfect!"

"Stunning, babes. Absolutely stunning."

"Let's put an offer in."

"Hold on. We've not seen inside yet."

"Don't need to. This is the place, Sarah. I can feel it."

Paul's impetuousness always worried Sarah; the way he instantly made his mind up about things was so different from her more thoughtful approach. It was like that when they first met. 'You're the one for me.' 'Let's get married.' 'I'm quitting my job and starting my own business.' 'I'm a winner, Sarah.'

Except for a few disasters along the way – like the 'genuine' Lowry he'd bought that turned out to be fake, oh and the dubious Spanish villa he'd purchased that was repossessed by the authorities as it was built on land set aside for conservation – most of the time his gut instinct had worked out. He did quit his job in IT to form his own successful software company. He had, as he'd predicted, become a 'winner.'

Pulling up outside the house Paul's heart began to race. "Oh wow! The kids are gonna love this place!" Staring at ivy-clad walls and large bay windows it was exactly the type of house he'd always dreamed of owning. It said so much about a person — successful, hard-working, someone with taste who wasn't afraid to push the boundaries. What he liked about the house was that it was conservative on the outside and ultra-modern within; the photos on the estate agent's website had convinced him to take a look — six en-suite bedrooms, sparkling marble kitchen, a quintet of spacious reception rooms filled with cutting-edge furniture, conservatory and outbuildings.

The front door opened and the estate agent came bouncing out, a beaming smile on his face. Paul and Sarah climbed out of their Range Rover.

"Welcome to Wren House. Beautiful property isn't it. And you've chosen the perfect day to view it."

Standing beneath a clear blue sky buffeted by a gentle February breeze Sarah couldn't agree more. The smell of sweet violets hung in the air as she took in the Victorian front porch with its freshly painted green door and gleaming brass door knocker.

The agent swept his hand beyond the beautifully manicured gardens and out towards gently sloping fields fringed by woodland. "Gorgeous view. The house comes with the ten acres, give or take… Right, let me show you around."

An hour or so later and the deal was done. Subject to contract, Wren House was theirs for five point eight million.

But there was a catch.

Sitting in the estate agent's office later that day he explained, "Now this may sound rather odd, and not a little off-putting. Situated within the grounds, though completely out of sight of the main house I might add, is a small cottage..."

"Brilliant!" exclaimed Paul. "We could turn it into a guest house or, or convert it into a gym."

"Or an office," added Sarah. "You could work from home more."

"What?" asked Paul, not listening.

The agent cut across them, smiling. "Sorry, if you'll just let me explain. This cottage is currently lived in by a couple who..."

Paul shot forward in his seat. "A couple? Well they'll just have to leave when we buy the place."

"Absolutely." agreed Sarah.

Again the agent gave a diplomatic smile. "It's not that simple, I'm afraid. The current owner will only go ahead with the sale if the buyer agrees to allow the couple to carry on living there."

Paul was gobsmacked. "What? I've never heard anything like it! Are they relatives or something?"

"Not as far as I know."

"Then who are they?"

"I'm not sure. It's the first time I've come across anything like this myself, so I'm just as much in the dark as you are. According to the current owner the couple are no trouble at all. They keep themselves to themselves. You'd hardly know they were there."

"Bloody outrageous!" said Paul. "How long have they been living there?"

The agent dug into the file. "Says here they've been tenants of the property now for... actually it doesn't. Must be a good few years."

The financial side of Paul's brain kicked in. "Tenants? That means they pay rent, right?"

The agent glanced at the file. "Peppercorn rent… Fifty pounds a year."

"Fifty quid a year? For a cottage in Cheshire! No way!"

"Written in stone I'm afraid."

"So what you're saying is, even if we buy the house, we can't kick them out or put the rent up?"

"That's correct... Not within the first year, anyhow."

"What's the first year got to do with anything?"

"According to clause thirteen of the contract, once you've lived there for a whole calendar year you can either renegotiate the rent or terminate the tenancy agreement."

Sarah looked at Paul hopefully. "That's something at least."

Paul shook his head. "A whole year? It's usually a month, isn't it?"

"That's correct," said the agent. "And I have to stress the current owners are particularly insistent upon this."

"Were they being blackmailed or something? Ridiculous!"

"Any chance we could have a word with the owners?" asked Sarah, trying to calm the situation. "Maybe they can put us in the picture."

"Sorry, they've gone to live abroad and have no wish to be contacted."

Paul threw his hands up. "Sod this!"

What the agent did next took them completely by surprise. He closed the file and got to his feet, bringing the meeting to a close. "Very well, I'll tell the owners you're not interested. Good afternoon."

Paul and Sarah left the estate agents in a state of shock.

Walking towards their car Paul vented his anger. "Can you believe the guy? We're paying almost six mil for a house only to be told we have to put up with a couple of scroungers. Well he can sod off!"

"It's only for a year."

"A year's a long time. Anything could happen. We might get robbed… or worse."

Sarah laughed. "You've been watching too many crime dramas Paul."

"I don't care. I am not putting with some deadbeats for a whole year."

As soon as they arrived home their two children — seventeen-year-old Tom and nineteen-year-old Jessica — pounced on them. They'd seen photos of Wren House and were eager to know how the viewing went. Both were desperate to move to a more prestigious property; Tom because he wanted to impress a girl at high school he was in love with, Jessica because most of her friends at college lived in much bigger houses than she did. One of them, Amelia, the daughter of a successful property developer, loved inviting Jessica over to her parent's mansion in Alderley Edge, smirking as she led her through room after opulent room. Jessica was sure that once she moved to larger house it would even things up within the group.

"You tell them about it," said Paul, heading out of the kitchen. "I need to phone Mike at the office."

Sarah grabbed a bottle of mineral water from the fridge. "Beautiful house, absolutely beautiful."

"Are we buying it then?" asked Jessica, eagerly.

"Are we?" added Tom, his eyes on stalks.

Sarah calmed them down and explained the situation about the cottage. Fuming that a couple of leaches were blocking their path to a better life, both kids let rip.

"Just buy the place, wait till they go shopping then burn the cottage down," said Tom. "End of story."

"Or I could ask a couple of scary guys I know from college to pay them a visit. They'd soon move out."

Sarah was both shocked and amused at her children's suggestions. "Plenty of other houses on the market. We'll just keep looking."

Paul was in the lounge on the phone to his business partner, Mike. Their IT company – InovaSystems -- had recently pitched to supply payroll software to a global engineering company. "Heard anything?"

Mike could barely suppress his delight. "Yeah, as a matter of fact... got a call from them this morning…"

Typical Mike, he loved dramatic pauses. "Just tell me."

"Looks like it's a yes."

"Really? Brilliant!"

"Hold on, Paul. It's not a done deal yet. There's still a few glitches to be ironed out. But overall they love the package. Our system's light years ahead of our competitors. I think they'll go for it."

It would be the biggest deal InovaSystems had pulled off since he and Mike formed the company eight years ago. Already Paul could see the business expanding; brand-new offices, state-of-the-art research facility, industry awards, not to mention an upswing in lifestyle. A glamorous movie began to play in his head featuring private jets, luxury hotels and tropical islands. Sarah was his co-star, laughing as they flitted around the globe from one exotic location to the next.

"How's the house-hunting going?" asked Mike.

"Don't ask."

Later that night, as Paul and Sarah lay in bed, Paul looked at her, his eyes full of regret. "Shame about Wren House. Perfect, wasn't it?"

Sarah placed her hand on his shoulder and gave it a gentle squeeze. "Forget it. We'll find somewhere just as nice."

But Paul couldn't forget it. Despite viewing several exclusive properties around Cheshire over the next few weeks, none of them came anywhere close to Wren House. There was something seductive about the place, made all the more frustrating by the fact that he himself had pulled the plug. Not that there was anything wrong with their current property — a four-bedroom detached house situated on an up market estate in Wilmslow — their dream home when they first bought it, and one they swore they would never tire of. But eventually, after living there for five years, the gloss had worn off and Paul began to get itchy feet.

As he kept insisting, "We've got tons more money now. We need a house that reflects our status."

Two

As February came to a close Paul finally received the news he'd been waiting for. He was about to drive off the first tee at Prestbury Golf Club when Mike rang. "Break out the shampers, bud. We've won the contract!"

Too excited to continue with the round he shoved his driver back in his golf bag and turned to his playing partners. "Sorry guys, you'll have to play without me."

A million thoughts swirled through his brain as he climbed into his Range Rover and headed home. He couldn't wait to tell Sarah and the kids. The look on their faces! Driving through Prestbury village the full realisation of the deal hit home. Over the next few years InovaSystems would earn millions. Not only that; when other companies got to hear how revolutionary their payroll system was, they too would want a piece of the action, meaning millions more would pour in through lucrative licensing agreements. Paul felt indestructible. A golden future lay ahead, all because of a simple algorithm he'd developed. *Nothing simple about it,* thought Paul. *You're a genius, mate.*

Paul waited until the family had gathered around the dinner table later that evening before breaking the news. There was stunned silence as Sarah, Jessica and Tom each worked out what it would mean for them. Jessica stood up and wrapped her arms around Paul's neck, peppering him with kisses. "Clever Daddy!" Already she could see racks of designer clothes filling the spacious walk-in wardrobe in her brand-new bedroom. Tom punched the air, "Yes!" certain that, once they'd moved to bigger house, which was now a given, his high school love interest would be putty in his hands. Sarah's eyes sparkled with joy. Paul looked round the table, revelling in the reaction of his family.

Who said money doesn't buy you happiness!

"What should we get Tom for his eighteenth?" asked Sarah. They were on their way to look at another house, their third viewing in a week.

"How about a new car? His old one keeps breaking down."

"Good idea."

"D'you know what I'd love to do? Get him a Porsche."

"*A Porsche!* Paul! He's far too young."

"Just a thought." He indicated left, turning into a shaded driveway. "What about an Audi TT? They're nice."

"Can we afford it?"

"Course we can."

"Are you sure?"

"I am *sure?* Sarah, I've just signed a deal worth millions."

The same estate agent who showed them Wren House was waiting patiently outside the front door of The Grange, a five-bedroom Neo-Georgian house on the outskirts of Alderley Edge. After a quick look round they decided it wasn't for them; it didn't have the character they were looking for, or the wow factor.

As the viewing came to an end Sarah asked, out of the blue, "Has Wren House been sold?"

"No," said the estate agent.

Paul scoffed. "I'm not surprised!"

"As a matter of fact it's under offer."

"Despite those deadbeats living in that cottage?"

The agent gave Paul a withering look. "I don't think the current owners would've put up with them if they were deadbeats."

Paul felt a twinge of regret at having missed out on the house of their dreams. Nothing he'd seen over the past month came anywhere close. And now another buyer – one who was obviously more open-minded and adventurous than him – was about to bag it.

Shit!

"Under offer, you say?" asked Paul, the cogs whirring.

"Yes," confirmed the estate agent.

The next day, on his way home from the office, Paul decided to pay another visit to Wren House. As he drove through the entrance gates he noticed the For Sale sign had been changed to Under Offer. His heart sank. He carried on up the drive. There was the house, bathed in afternoon sunlight. It was even lovelier than before. Paul imagined showing his friends round.

Oh yes. They'd be well impressed.

Paul stopped in front of the house. Climbing out

of his Range Rover he gazed towards the fringe of woodland, behind which, according the estate agent, lay the cottage. Paul knew what to do. He walked through the ornamental garden until he came to a small wooden gate that opened onto a field. He pushed open the gate and strolled through ankle-deep grass. Strange. He hardly ever felt nervous. But now, as he approached the entrance to the woods, his heat began to race.

Making his way through the trees he was stunned by the receding carpet of bluebells lining the forest floor, punctuated here and there by the occasional crop of daffodils. Eventually he caught sight of the cottage. Built of Cheshire brick, with tiny windows and a slate roof topped by a single chimney, it sat serenely in its woodland setting. Surrounding the cottage was a wooden fence enclosing a tiny garden packed with wild flowers, not that Paul knew what any of them were. Nevertheless the splash of colour took his breath away. As he got closer he noticed half a dozen chickens pecking around the front door. To the right of the cottage was a well-stocked kitchen garden. Paul could see rows and rows of neatly hoed beds ready for planting. Beyond a rickety shed and slanting greenhouse a rough track led off into the woods. The estate agent was right on both counts; the cottage was well away from the main house, and the tenants were far from deadbeats. Standing at the garden gate Paul noticed the cottage was slightly run down – the brickwork needed re-pointing and the front door and window frames could do with of a lick of paint.

He took a deep breath and walked up the path. Through an open downstairs window came the faint sound of a 1940's crooner backed by the soft tones of a palm court orchestra. *Who the hell lives here?* He pictured a grey-haired couple in their eighties huddled round a gramophone.

Paul coughed nervously as he tapped on the front door. The muffled sound of a dog barking. Footsteps. The front door creaked open. A tall, slim man dressed in brown corduroy trousers, checked shirt and a Fair Isle tank top stood there smiling. Old fashioned or trendy? It was hard to tell. As was his age. Balding, with a broad, friendly face and high forehead, he reminded Paul of one of those soldiers from the First World War who looked forty but were barely eighteen.

"Come in! Come in!" said the man, throwing open the door like he'd known Paul forever. "I'm Jack... Grace! We've got a visitor!"

A delighted female voice sounded from the kitchen. "Ooh! I'll put the kettle on."

The dog was just as welcoming, jumping up and wagging its tail.

Paul winced.

"Down, Jess! Don't be ruining the man's nice suit now."

"Thanks," said Paul, brushing an imaginary paw mark from the top of his trousers. "Made to measure. Cost a fortune."

"Sorry about that... Come in and make yourself at home. Tea?"

"Err… yes please. Milk, no sugar."

"Right you are. Shan't be a mo'." Jack left the room.

Paul looked around. He couldn't believe how threadbare and out-of-date everything was. The tiny room was beyond basic – cast iron fireplace, 1950's sideboard, sunken bottle-green couch and matching armchair, gold-tasselled standard lamp, and a worm-eaten bookcase packed with paperbacks. No TV, no computer, the only form of entertainment an old transistor radio perched on the sideboard. Paul shook his head. *Imagine living like this! The poor sods.*

Sinking into the armchair he noticed how spotlessly clean everything was; a far cry from what he imagined when the estate agent first told him about the mysterious couple living in the cottage; a violent roughneck and his blousy wife came to mind, with a vicious Alsatian tied up outside surrounded by broken-down cars. *Just goes to show.*

"Here we are!"

A middle aged lady wearing a long floral dress presented him with a cup of tea and a scone. "You timed that well. Just come out of the oven."

"Thanks," said Paul.

The lady was petite, with short brown hair and large hazel eyes. Her skin was flawless, without a trace of make-up.

"This is my wife, Grace.," announced Jack, walking back into the room.

"Hi, Grace. I'm Paul."

"Lovely to meet you, Paul. You must be the husband of the lady who visited last week; the one who's put an offer in for Wren House. She said you'd come and see us."

"No, no. I viewed the house about a month ago. I'm interested in buying it though. The estate agent told me about you, so I thought I'd drop by and say hello."

"Oh!" said Grace. "So *you* might be buying it? Well, I don't blame you. It's a lovely house. You'll have to be quick, mind. The lady's set her heart on the place."

"Really?"

"Anyway, tuck in." said Jack, noticing the worried look on Paul's face. "If it's meant to be it's meant to be."

"You should have seen them, Sarah. Talk about mousey. And you should see the way they live! Like going back in time. They don't even have central heating. God knows how they get on in the winter. They'd be better off in a council flat."

"Did you ask them why the rent's so cheap?"

"Of course I didn't."

"Why not? It's a perfectly reasonable question. Remember what happened with that house in Spain?"

One thing Paul hated was being reminded of past mistakes. "It doesn't matter how cheap the rent is, does it?" he snapped, 'If we don't let them live there we can't buy the place. Simple as that… Anyway, like you said, it's only for a year. "

"True."

"It's far from perfect, Sarah, I know that. But

having met the couple they seem all right to me. Besides, they live way off in the woods, so we'd never see them."

Sarah stared at the carpet. A picture of Wren House floated into her mind. It really was idyllic. If the couple were okay then why not put up with the situation? She raised her head and looked at Paul. "OK. Let's go for it."

"Brilliant, babes. You won't regret it."

"Hold on. The house is under offer. Say it's been accepted?"

Paul smiled. "I've already put in a bid for fifty K above the asking price. The house is as good as ours."

"What? You've put in an offer without telling me?"

Paul grinned cheekily. "You snooze you lose, Sarah."

Three

The arguments began the moment they moved in! "I'm having this bedroom!" screamed Jessica.

"No you're not!"

"Yes I am! I've got tons more clothes than you. *And* I'm older."

Tom ran out onto the landing and leaned over the banister. "Mum! Jessica's being a bitch. She wants the best bedroom. Tell her she can't have it."

Sarah was busy dealing with the removal men; one of them had dropped a box marked 'fragile', smashing part of a dinner service they'd bought in New York.

"Look at it!" she yelled, staring into the box. "It's ruined!"

"Mum!"

"Shut up, Tom!" She turned to the head removal man. "I want compensating for this."

"I'm sorry, madam. If you'd like to phone head office and put in a claim, I'm sure they'll sort it out."

"Too bloody right I will."

An hour later and the removal men were gone.

Sarah was in one of the receptions rooms at the back of the house unpacking when Paul appeared clutching a bottle of champagne and a bunch of roses.

She glanced at him angrily. "Fancy leaving me to cope on my own. Talk about stressed."

Paul put the champagne on the coffee table, rushed over and gave her a hug. "Sorry, hun. The meeting took longer than expected. Anyway I'm back now." He handed her the roses. "These are for you."

Her tense features softened. "Orr, thanks."

Paul glanced at the pile of boxes littering the room. So much stuff. Where had it all come from? He clapped his hands. "Right. Let's get this lot unpacked."

"I'll do down here. You start upstairs?"

"Sure."

"And sort Tom out. He's sulking because Jessica's bagged the biggest bedroom."

"Well she is the eldest."

"That's what I told him."

Paul walked up the curved wooden staircase, savouring his new surroundings. He couldn't believe the house was theirs at last. It had only taken a month, but it seemed like forever. He walked down the landing and peered into each passing bedroom. At the end of the landing was the main bedroom. Next door he found Tom lying on his bed talking on his mobile. As soon as Tom set eyes on him he ended the call and jumped up.

"Dad? How come Jessica's got..."

"Because that's the way things are. When I was young your auntie Claire got the best bedroom." Paul stepped inside and looked around. "Anyway, what are you bothered about? It's nice in here." He walked to the window and looked out. "Great view."

"Yeah but her room's bigger."

"This is hardly a shoebox, Tom. Bloody hell. It's

twice the size of your old one."

"Yeah but hers is bigger."

"Listen," said Paul, getting more and more frustrated. "Get the rest of your stuff unpacked and don't be such a wuss!"

Tom stared at the carpet; Sarah's trait. "Yes, Dad."

"When you've finished, go downstairs and give your mother a hand."

By the time everything had been unpacked and put away it was gone 8 p.m. For the first proper meal in their new home Sarah had planned to cook, but tiredness and the lateness of the hour forced a change of plan, so Paul rang the local Chinese restaurant and asked them to deliver.

As it was such a lovely evening Sarah decided they would eat out on the patio. With views across the ornamental garden and out towards open fields it was picture-perfect.

As the sun went down and the family tucked into their banquet for four, Paul looked around him and sighed. "Bliss."

Everyone agreed. They were so excited to be in their new home that the stresses of the day seemed to melt away. They really had to pinch themselves — life couldn't get any better, surely?

"It's so peaceful," said Sarah. "Not like our old house."

Jessica topped up her glass of white wine. "Oh my God, right. Can you *imagine* what it's like there tonight! Tim'll be barbecuing. Diane'll be pissed, and the kids'll be running around screaming. Nightmare."

Paul laughed. "I'm so glad we're out of there."

The sound of a dog barking deep within the woods.

"What's that?" asked Tom.

"Jack's dog, probably?" said Paul. "Hey! It's got the same name as you Jess. When you get chance, go over and meet them."

"No way… Have you met them yet, Mum?"

Sarah shook her head. "Not yet."

"Not the dog," said Tom, pointing. "That there."

Paul glanced over at a large stone lion in the centre of the ornamental garden. "Oh that. It's a fountain."

"Really." said Sarah. "Switch it on. It'll be nice to hear splashing water."

"It doesn't work. I tried earlier... I'll get someone in to fix it."

"When?"

"When I get chance."

"When will that be?"

Quick to detect the first rumblings of an argument Jessica changed the subject. "It's your eighteenth in two weeks Tom. Excited?"

"Can't wait. I'll finally be able to drink."

"Do me favour." laughed Sarah.

Tom blushed, "Legally, I mean."

Paul got up from the table. "In that case..." he wandered into the kitchen and returned with a chilled bottle of Moët and four champagne flutes. "May as well start as we mean to go on." Peeling the gold foil Paul expertly popped the cork. Filling all four glasses to the brim he handed them out. "Cheers everyone!

Here's to our new home!"

"Cheers!"

Paul took a sip of champagne. A feeling of contentment washed over him. He glanced towards the woods — he pictured Tom and Grace sitting in their run-down cottage listening to the radio.

Poor sods

By the time Paul came downstairs for breakfast the next morning Sarah was already in the kitchen drinking coffee.

"Morning babes. You're up early." he said, yawning. "Big day ahead. I need a man-size breakfast."

Sarah got up and walked towards the fridge. "Full English?"

"Brilliant." Paul sat down. "Really weird. When I woke up this morning I thought I was back in our old house. Then I looked out the window and realised I wasn't. Was I relieved."

"I know what you mean. I got up at six and went for a walk around the garden. So lovely."

"We're going to be happy here, Sarah. I can feel it."

Sarah took the bacon and eggs from the fridge, splashed oil into a pan and placed it on the cooker. "Oh, by the way, the lock on the back door sticks. Can we get someone in to fix it? Took me ages to open it this morning."

First the fountain, now this.

"Disaster."

"I don't mean now, Paul. When you get chance."

"Leave it with me… Will you ring the marquee people? Won't have time. Need to pop to the Audi garage and sort out Tom's TT."

Sarah placed three slices of whole meal bread under the grill. "Can't help thinking we're storing up trouble."

"What do you mean?"

"With the car. When Jessica sees it she's bound to want a new one. It's her birthday next month, don't forget."

"Never mind. We'll buy her one as well."

☯

Desperate for some fresh air Paul made his way out of the marquee. Threading his way between tables he felt someone grab his arm; it was his business partner Mike, a sweaty, drunken look on his face.

"Hey, Paul. Great party."

"What?"

"GREAT PARTY!"

"Oh yeah. Cheers. Bloody music's too loud."

"You're getting old, mate."

"I feel it."

Paul noticed Mike's table was littered with empty champagne bottles. Sitting next to him was a beautiful twenty-something blonde girl wearing a low-cut gold dress. Paul leaned in gave him a nudge. "Bit young for you, isn't she?"

Mike smiled, "You're only jealous."

Mike was well-known around the office as a

womaniser, he had every dating app under the sun on his iPhone. Usually he went out with women his own age. Recently, however, since the business had taken off and the money was rolling in, they were a lot younger. And a lot more attractive. As well as upgrading his women Mike had upgraded his car – gone was the BMW 5 Series, replaced by a sleek black Ferrari. Paul put this down to a mid-life crisis. Although Mike was two years older he was more like a younger brother. Every Monday he would rush into Paul's office and show him photos of the various women he'd dated over the weekend. Real stunners some of them. Staring at the litany of busty cleavages and pouting lips, Paul wondered if he was missing out.

Mike put his arm around the blonde girl. "This is Amy. Gorgeous, isn't she? Amy, meet my business partner Paul. The guy's a genius."

Amy stared at Paul. "Mike's told me all about you. He didn't tell me how fit you were, though. You kept that quiet, Mike."

"Hands off," joked Mike, "He's married. That's his wife cavorting on the dance floor."

"Pity." Swaying, Amy got to her feet. "Dance with me, Paul. Let's make her jealous."

"Sorry, I don't dance. Anyway I need some fresh air. Not stopped since this morning."

Amy crashed back into her seat. "Whatever."

Paul smiled at Mike as if to say, you've got your hands full there mate, then walked outside. He took a deep lungful of cool evening air and made his way to the ornamental garden. Tipsy, he sat down on a stone bench next to the fountain. He still hadn't got round to getting it fixed. Next week, he promised himself. Paul looked at his watch: 10:44. It had been a long day — up at seven to take delivery of the Audi TT, he then dragged Tom out of bed and led him blindfold down the stairs and out of the house for the big unveiling. Tom's face when he opened his eyes and saw the car. Priceless. As anticipated Jessica started sulking, following him around all morning saying she wanted a brand-new Mercedes for *her* birthday. In the end, to stop her winging, he said yes, and she ran off whooping. Just as things were calming down the marquee people arrived – a day late – then the caterers. Talk about stress! Despite that, everything had fallen into place. Tom was happy, Jess was happy, and it was great party. So in the end it was all worthwhile.

Paul leaned back and gazed at the stars. It was a lovely evening, a three-quarter moon hanging lazily in the sky. The perfect end to a perfect day. Behind him he could hear the thump! thump! of the music.

Thank God I don't have any neighbours.

Then he remembered Jack and Grace.

No sweat. They're too far away to hear.

Paul was seized by an uncontrollable desire to go to the cottage. Ever since he'd moved to Wren House he kept comparing his luxurious surroundings with the threadbare hovel in the woods. Not out of any sense of guilt or shame, but for the sheer joy of appreciating how much he'd achieved. Maybe that was the reason the previous owners had allowed Jack and Grace to live there; they were a constant reminder never to take things for granted.

Clever.

A shooting star shot across the sky.

Go on, go to the cottage. Have a quick look. You deserve it. The perfect end to the perfect day.

Without thinking he got to his feet, opened the little wooden gate and set out across the field. Above the tree-line he noticed the Plough constellation arcing across the sky. He reached the edge of the field and peered into the gloom. Darkness enfolded the woods. He picked his way carefully between the trees until he came to the clearing. There was the cottage, cloaked in shadow, a single downstairs light shining through a crack in the curtains. Although he'd been here before the sight still shocked him. It looked so remote and out of touch. It was hard to believe anyone would choose to live there. Then his cynicism kicked in.

Mind you, for fifty quid a year who wouldn't?

A rustle of leaves to his right made him jump. It was a badger. Stopping to sniff the air it eyed him suspiciously before scuttling off into woods. Paul had never seen a badger before, except lying dead by the roadside.

He walked down a shallow incline thick with ferns until he came to the gate. Lifting the latch carefully he pushed it open. The hinges creaked. *Shit!* He froze; worried Jess might start barking… He carried on up the path. To the left of the front door he could see the downstairs window illuminated from within. Tiptoeing, he edged past the porch and crouched beneath the sill. He could hear the faint crackle of the radio. Otherwise the room was silent. Overcome with the desire to look inside he inched himself up and peered through the crack in the curtains. Jack was sitting in the armchair reading a book, Jess at his feet. Grace was relaxing on the sofa, knitting. It was exactly what he expected. Nevertheless the ordinariness of the scene touched him.

Walking back across the field towards the marquee he realised his night-time adventure had backfired. What kind of a person was he, spying on an impoverished couple just to make himself feel good? He hated to admit it, but deep down he felt on top of the world.

Four

Over the next few months Paul made a habit of visiting the cottage, though this time during the day. Whenever he was fed up – like the time Jessica backed her brand-new Mercedes into a lamp post the day after her birthday, or when Tom came home late one night and threw up on the lounge carpet — he would wander over for a chat. Drinking tea in the little stone-floored kitchen with its gnarled wooden table and cast iron range, all the stresses and strains of the day seemed to melt away. Jack and Grace were great company. They asked him all sorts questions; about his life, his business, his family. He got so engrossed in the conversation he would lose track of time, often arriving home late for dinner. As well as having a good moan it gave Paul the opportunity to boast — how much his new conservatory was costing, the diamond bracelet he'd surprised Sarah with the other night at a fancy restaurant they'd probably never heard of, or the once-in-a-lifetime holiday he was planning for her 40th birthday.

"The Burj Al Arab in Dubai. Seven star job. You do not wanna *know* how much that cost!"

"Ooh! How lovely!" said Grace.

Paul helped himself to another slice of walnut cake. "Are you going away this summer?"

"Not been away for years," said Jack. "We have

the odd day out now and again — Tatton Park, Buxton — but we love it here, don't we, Grace?"

Grace leaned across the table and squeezed Jack's hand, her hazel eyes shining. "We do, Jack."

Paul couldn't believe what he was hearing. *They probably can't afford a holiday and are too embarrassed to admit it.* He also found it strange that, no matter how much he bragged about his family's privileged lifestyle, they never seemed to get jealous. Just the opposite. They were thrilled. But what *really* got on his nerves was how affectionate they were with each other.

Like a couple of newly-weds.

One day he was chatting with Jack in the kitchen garden when he asked, "Are you any good at DIY?"

Jack had just lifted a forkful of potatoes from the ground and was staring at them, mesmerised.

"Jack?"

"Sorry." Jack stood up, straightening his back. "I can put my hand to most things, why?"

"Got a small plumbing job. You know the fountain in the ornamental garden?"

"The stone lion? Yes."

"It's not worked since the day we moved in. My wife keeps going on about it. You've not met Sarah, have you?"

"I haven't, no."

"When she wants something done she goes on and on about it. Pain in the arse sometimes… Anyway, do you think you could fix it?"

"I'll give it a go."

"Brilliant. You've saved my life. When can you

come over?"

"How about tomorrow morning?"

"Great stuff. What time?"

"Eight o'clock."

"Early bird, eh? That's what we like to hear."

The next morning Paul decided to work from home. He'd set up an office in one of the spare bedrooms overlooking the ornamental garden and sure enough, at 7:58, he saw Jack making his way across the field carrying his tool bag.

"Bang on time," he said to Sarah, who was just passing the door clutching the laundry basket.

"Ooh!" Sarah dropped the basket and rushed into Paul's office. "Let's have a look at him then." She got to the window just as Jack was opening the little wooden gate. "So you're our mysterious neighbour, are you? Love the flat cap. Very trendy… Hey! He's not bad looking."

"Don't get any ideas, Lady Chatterley!"

She watched as Jack put his tool bag down and removed his cap. "Oh no, he's going bald. I'm not into bald men."

"Women! You're so fickle."

"I've stayed with you, haven't I?"

He slapped her bottom playfully. "Cheeky!"

Throughout the morning Paul kept looking up from his desk as Jack set about trying to repair the fountain. First he cleaned the inside of the lion's mouth with a wire brush. Then, after inspecting the valve at the base of the fountain, he dug a small trench to check the pipe work. An hour later, Paul saw Sarah walk into the ornamental garden with a mug of tea and a plate of biscuits. Polite as ever, Jack took his cap off as she approached. They had a brief chat. At one point he heard Sarah howl with laughter.

Paul was kept busy answering calls, writing emails and taking a virtual meeting with Mike and a couple of software engineers. Apparently there was a problem with the payroll system. Nothing serious. At lunchtime he was just about to head downstairs when he saw Grace emerge from the woods carrying a wicker basket. She walked across the field, opened the little wooden gate and made her way to the fountain. When Jack saw her he gave her a peck on the cheek and they both sat down on the stone bench. Jack delved into the basket, removing a tartan Thermos flask and a brown paper bag. He opened the bag and looked inside, smelling the contents. His face lit up. He took out a handful of sandwiches — his favourite, obviously — and set them on his knee. As he did so, Grace unscrewed the top of the flask and poured out two cups of tea. Paul watched as they sat eating their lunch, blissful in each other's company.

"I'm starving," announced Paul, walking into the kitchen. "I could eat a—" his heart sank when he read the note on the marble worktop. 'Having lunch in Knutsford with the girls. There's some chicken legs in the fridge. See you later. x'.

It was around 3 p.m. when Paul looked up from his desk and saw water spurting from the lion's mouth.

Well, the clever sod.

He got up and rushed outside to find Jack replacing the squares of turf he'd removed to dig the trench.

"Hey. Well done."

Jack smiled modestly. "Working fine now."

"Looks great. What was the problem?"

"A couple of leaks in the pipe. Soon as I soldered them the water pressure rose and Bob's your uncle."

"Can't thank you enough. Really. Sarah'll be thrilled… How much do I owe you?"

"Oh, give us twenty quid."

"Twenty quid! Jack! You've been here most of the day." Paul took out his wallet and gave him two fifty pound notes. "Here."

Jack was stunned. "Are you sure?"

"Course I'm sure. You've worked hard. Take it."

"Thanks. Thanks very much."

As Jack bent down to gather up his tools Paul asked, "You're obviously a plumber?"

"No, no. I used to be a gardener before I retired."

"Retired! You don't look old enough."

"Thanks... Oh, while I remember." Jack pointed to a nearby trellis. "Tell your gardener to prune the clematis before autumn sets in. You'll have a lot more flowers next year."

"Will do." Paul suddenly remembered another job that needed doing. "Before you go Jack, would you mind taking a look at the back door? The lock keeps sticking. It's driving Sarah mad."

"Ah, I know what that is. Graham used to have the same problem."

"Graham?"

"The chap who lived here before you. Hold on." He delved into his tool bag and removed a can of WD40. "Right. Let the dog see the rabbit."

They set off towards the house. It was the chance Paul had been waiting for. "You got on well with the last owner then? Graham?"

"*Very* well, yes. He was nice man. So was his wife, Carla. Similar to you in many ways."

"Good of you to say… So err, when did you start renting the cottage off them?"

"We didn't. We were already living there when they bought the place. We've lived there for years... Right, this is the offending door, I believe. It's quite simple." Jack spayed WD40 into the lock, took hold of the door handle and began levering it up and down. "Buy yourselves a can of this. When it sticks, just spray the inside of the lock and give the handle a good old yank. That's what Graham used to do. You won't have any trouble after that."

"That's brilliant, Jack. Thanks."

Later that evening Paul and Sarah were sitting in the ornamental garden admiring the fountain.

Sarah took a sip of wine. "Makes such a difference now its working."

"Really nice, yeah." Paul refilled his glass of Barolo and stared across at the woods. "Strange set-up?"

"What is?"

"Jack and Grace living in the cottage. When I asked him how long they've been living there he just said 'for years'… Bloody strange set-up. Anyway, what did you think of him?"

"Jack? Oh he's *so* nice; one of those old fashioned gentlemen."

"I saw you talking to him. What did he say?"

"Not much. He said his wife was knitting him a jumper for winter. I told the girls over lunch and they all burst out laughing. Imagine Tilly doing that! I *don't* think."

Paul couldn't help himself. "Imagine you doing it."

"Precisely!"

Deep down Paul was stung.

"Still, it'd give you something to do while we're in Dubai."

"Dubai?"

Paul removed a brochure from his back pocket and gave it to Sarah. Confused, she stared at the glossy photo of the Burj Al Arab, its sail-like structure rising out of the desert. "What's this?"

"Your birthday present."

It took a moment to sink in. "What? Are you... taking me here?"

"I sure am."

"OH MY GOD! Really?" She flung her arms around his neck. "Oh thank you thank you thank you!"

Five

The quad bike's rear tyres dug into the hot sand causing the front of the chassis to tip violently. *Bloody hell!* Paul leaned forward and eased off the accelerator. Cresting the top of the enormous sand dune the sight that greeted him was breathtaking: from horizon to horizon there was nothing but dessert, mile upon rippling mile.

"Magnificent, no?" asked the guide.

Before he had chance to speak the rest of the tour group answered as one. "Wonderful, Mohammed!"

Paul looked down into the valley. He could see a group of air-conditioned SUVs surrounding a large encampment where various activities were taking place – falconry, belly dancing, henna art, sand-boarding. Something for everyone. But not for Sarah.

So far their four-day holiday had been an amazing experience — flying first class, a limo to the Burj Al Arab, the unbelievable luxury of their hotel suite, the food, the shopping, the night-life. Paul had never seen Sarah look so happy, especially last night over dinner when he gave her a diamond-encrusted Rolex for her birthday. But this morning when he told her about the trip he'd booked the atmosphere suddenly changed.

"It's our last full day today, Paul. The last thing I want to do is go to the desert. It's boiling!" she'd moaned as she snatched a hair clip off the dressing table. "You're always arranging things without telling me."

Paul wanted to say, 'Like this holiday, you mean,' but he didn't.

"You know I hate outdoor stuff… Anyway, you promised me we'd go to the perfume museum."

"I'm sick of air-conditioned rooms. I want some fresh air… Besides, we've spent the last three days doing what you want to do."

"Well it is *my* birthday."

"I know it is. I just wanna do something different, that's all."

Sarah realised it was useless to argue. Once Paul had made his mind up that was that, birthday or no birthday. "OK! OK! I'll go. But don't expect me get on a bloody camel."

When Paul and the rest of the group rode back into camp there was a belly dancing class taking place on a small, makeshift stage. An Arab lady was giving a demonstration, her hips shimmering beneath her gauzy, see-through dress. Surrounding her were around twenty tourists clapping and cheering. Paul got off the quad bike and walked towards the stage. That's when he noticed Sarah; she was sitting apart from the group, a miserable look on her face.

Shit... Keep calm, Paul. Keep calm.

"Oh my God, Sarah. You should see the view from the top of the dunes!" He squinted into the sun and pointed to the topmost dune a kilometre away. "We were *right* up there. On that one. Amazing!"

Sarah gave a cursory glance and said, with no

enthusiasm whatsoever, "Great."

"What've you been doing?"

She wanted to say, 'I've been stuck in this baking heat for the past two hours with a load of morons.' Instead she got to her feet, brushing sand off her dress. "Watching the falconry display."

"Any good?"

She glared at him. "A bird flew around in the sky, Paul!"

They spent their last evening having dinner in the Al Muntaha, one of the Burj Al Arab's most iconic restaurants. The atmosphere was subdued, despite the feigned enthusiasm. Paul glanced across at Sarah. Hidden behind her smile was a sadness he'd never seen before. She looked up and noticed Paul's tense expression. She averted her gaze, letting it come to rest on the diamond-encrusted Rolex he'd given her the previous night. Must have cost a fortune. So had the holiday. A wave of guilt swept over her. Why had she been so obnoxious after he'd spent all that money?

Fingering her napkin she looked up. "I've had a lovely time, Paul. Thanks ever so much."

During the flight home Paul noticed Sarah was drinking more than usual. Every time the steward came round to refresh everyone's champagne flutes she stopped him and asked him to pour. By the time they got back to the UK she was glassy-eyed and slurring.

Two weeks later Paul received some wonderful news. "Profits for the last quarter have tripled," announced Mike excitedly.

"Tripled! Are you sure?"

"Just got off the phone to our accountants. Nearly fell off my chair when they told me. Amazing isn't it?" Paul could almost hear Mike's mind whirring. Sure enough. "I'm thinking of buying a new house. Something grand like yours. What are you going to buy?"

His own thoughts weren't far behind. "Bentley GT. Definitely."

"*Nice!* And I'm definitely buying a house in France. Always wanted a place in France… We've made it, bud. We're big league now." Paul put the phone down. He was ecstatic.

"Sar—"

He suddenly remembered she'd gone to Chester Races with the girls and both his children were staying at their new holiday home in Abersoch, so he had no one to share the wonderful news with. Staring through the window towards the woods he suddenly remembered Jack and Grace. Of course! Why not pay them a visit? He rushed downstairs into the kitchen. Opening the fridge he took out a chilled bottle of Dom Pérignon.

They won't have tasted this baby before!

Keen to celebrate he dashed out of the house and headed across the field. As he strolled through the woods Paul felt on top of the world; there was so much he could do with his new-found wealth — cars, clothes, holidays — the list was endless. He pictured himself driving into Prestbury Golf Club in his spanking new Bentley GT — *black*, he decided, *more gravitas* — and seeing the look on the member's faces.

Oh yes, I'm big league now.

He caught sight of the cottage through the trees. After weeks of visiting Jack and Grace the picture of domestic bliss that always greeted him was beginning to grate.

It's probably just an act and they hate each other's guts? Jack's hardly the best provider. Grace must be sick of wearing the same old clothes and going to boring places like Buxton. I mean, Buxton for heaven's sake!

He was overtaken by the desire to sneak up on them in the hope of witnessing a domestic bust-up. Approaching the gate he hid behind a tree. Voices came from the back of the cottage. Raised voices! A man and a woman's!

"You're a bloody nightmare, lady!"

"Don't talk to me like that. You're a bully! Always have been!"

Bloody hell! Thought so!

Secretly delighted he moved in an arc, dashing from one tree to the next, until the rear of the cottage came into view. Jack and Grace were sitting on a bench outside the back door. Both were hunched forward, tension gripping their bodies.

Here we go.

"I wish I'd never married you! D'you know that!"

"Sod off to your fancy woman, then! That's right, I know all about her!"

"You know nothing, Ruth!"

Ruth?

The theme tune from *The Archers* filled the woods. Jack and Grace leaned back, delighted looks on their faces.

"I knew he was up to no good," said Grace, rising to her feet and switching off the radio.

"You were right, love."

"I can't wait for the next episode. Cup of tea?"

"Love one."

Paul watched Jack and Grace walk inside and close the door. Ashamed, he hid behind the tree for a while before making his way to the front of the cottage. He opened the gate, walked up the path and knocked at the door, setting Jess off barking. Moments later Jack answered. "Hello, Paul. Come in. Did you have a nice holiday?"

Paul entered. "Amazing."

"Cup of tea?"

"Sod the tea." He lifted the bottle of Dom. "Let's have a glass of bubbly. I'm celebrating."

"Grace!"

They both walked into the kitchen to find Grace standing at the kitchen table easing a ball of dough into a baking tin, her dark blue pinny dusted with flour.

"Look what Paul's brought round to drink."

Grace wiped her hands on a tea towel. "Ooh! Champagne!"

"He's celebrating."

"Why, what's happened?"

"Just had a call from my business partner." He tore off the silver foil around the neck of the bottle. "Get the glasses Jack."

"Will do!"

"The company's profits have tripled during the last quarter."

"That *is* good news," beamed Grace. "You must be thrilled."

"Just a bit."

"Will these do?" asked Jack, pulling three glass tumblers of various sizes from the Welsh dresser. "Sorry, they're all we've got."

"Don't apologise, they're perfect."

Jack set the tumblers down on the kitchen table as Paul popped the cork.

"Oooh!" exclaimed Grace.

"Best sound in the world," Paul laughed and, as he poured the champagne, a rainbow of bubbles crested the rim of each glass. "Cheers, everyone!"

"Cheers!"

"Ooh that's nice," said Grace, taking a sip. "Bubbles go right up your nose."

Jack agreed. "Umm, lovely… Let's go in the front room."

"I'll join you in a second," said Grace, picking up the baking tin. "Just need to put this in the oven."

Paul followed Jack into the front room and plonked himself in the armchair. "Tell you what, Jack. Paid a fortune for my armchair: Italian. Nowhere near as comfy as this."

Jack sat on the sofa. Smiling, he patted Jess on the

head. "That old thing. We've had it years. Well worn in, I suppose... I was just saying to Paul, Grace; we've had our furniture for years."

Grace smiled proudly. "We certainly have."

"I wish my wife was like that. Every five minutes she wants to change things; new sofa, new curtains."

Grace sat next to Jack. "Did she enjoy Dubai, your wife? Sarah, isn't it?"

"That's right." Paul took a swig of champagne. "Oh she loved it, yeah. We had a great time. Superb."

"You'll be having plenty more holidays in future now your business is doing so well."

"Umm." Paul stared into space wistfully. "Can I ask you something, Grace?"

"Of course."

"When you go to Buxton, what do you do?"

"What do we *do?*" She looked at Jack, confused. "Well now, let's see… we walk round the shops, have tea in a little café we know."

Jack nodded. "Nice place. Clean. Does a lovely cream tea."

"Don't forget the homemade chocolate cake." Grace glanced at Paul. "Jack's favourite."

"Best I've ever tasted." Jack squeezed Grace's hand. "Sorry, love."

"I forgive you."

"Then what do you do, after you've been in the café?"

"If the weather's nice we go to the Pavilion Gardens and listen to the brass band. It's so relaxing, sitting in the deckchairs."

"I always ask the band-leader to play 'Yesterday'," said Jack. "Grace's favourite."

"Great song." Paul drilled deeper. "What happens if it's raining?"

"That's easy. We go in the glasshouse."

"Beautiful Victorian conservatory," said Grace. "Very historic. It has palm trees and everything. And the heat! Like being abroad. Not that we've ever been abroad."

"Is it expensive to go in?"

"Not at all. It's free."

Jack nudged Grace. "Hey, do you remember the time we caught that little boy peeing behind a giant fern?"

Grace burst out laughing. "Oh it was so funny, Paul. Really. You should have seen his little face."

"Well you know what they say," smirked Jack. "When you've got to go you've got to go."

"We laughed about it all the way home. Tickles me even now… Anyway, enough about our boring day out. We want to hear about *your* holiday, Paul."

Paul went to refresh their glasses.

"Oh no thanks," said Jack, placing his hand over his glass. "I've got work to do in the garden later."

Grace did the same. "I won't either, if that's alright. This one's gone *straight* to my head."

Paul topped up his glass and was about to launch into what an amazing time he and Sarah had had when his mobile rang. "'Scuse me." He looked at the screen which read 'Jessica'.

"Hi, Jess. How's the weather in Abersoch?" He

put his hand over the phone, glancing smugly at Jack and Grace. "We've just bought a place in Abersoch."

Jack and Grace smiled and nodded.

Paul put the phone back to his ear. His daughter was sobbing.

"Jess? What's wrong?"

"It… it's Tom. He's been arrested."

"Arrested! What for?"

"Assault."

"Assault!"

Shocked, Jack and Grace stared at one another. To give Paul some privacy they got up and walked into the kitchen.

"Who's he assaulted?"

"Becky."

"Who's Becky?"

"A girl from high school he's obsessed with."

"He's assaulted a *girl!* For heaven's sake! What's *she* doing there? It was only supposed to be the two of you!"

"I know, but he…"

"Never mind. Where is he now?"

"Pwllheli police station." Overwhelmed, Jessica burst into tears. "Oh Dad, he's in a terrible state."

"Where are you?"

"I'm at the police station."

Paul jumped to his feet. "Right! Stay there. I'm on my way. And tell Tom to keep his mouth shut."

Frantic, he rushed into the kitchen. Jack and Grace were standing by the back door, tense looks on their faces.

"Sorry. I've got to go."

"Of course," said Grace. "We understand."

Paul put his head in his hands. "Oh God." An overwhelming anger erupted inside him. "Bloody kids!"

Paul dashed into the front room. Rushing towards the door he accidentally kicked over the bottle of Dom Pérignon. "Shit!" For a spit second he watched the fizzing liquid seep into the carpet. He yanked open the door and ran into the woods, yelling into his phone, "Mark Jordan!" A split second later his lawyer's voice came on the line.

"Paul. What can I—"

"Get to Pwllheli police station right now. My son's been arrested for assault... Yeah, yeah, I'm just about to set off. See you there."

Blasting down the M56 he rang Jessica to get the full story.

"Tom invited her without telling me. He's absolutely besotted, but she's not interested. I tried telling him but he wouldn't listen... Oh Dad, you should have heard him showing off — my family are rich, look at my car, look at my jet ski. It was pathetic. Anyway, last night we all went to the pub and Becky got off with this lad. Really fit he was. Tom went apeshit and stormed out. She got back to the house about an hour ago. They had a huge row. Tom called her a whore and punched her in the face. She ran outside crying and rang the police. Ten minutes later this cop car pulls up and Tom gets arrested... It was awful, Dad."

When Paul arrived at Pwllheli police station Jessica ran outside and gave him a hug. "He's been released on bail."

"That's something… Go and wait in the car, Jess."

He walked inside to find a dishevelled Tom standing at the custody desk with Mark Jordan, who was signing the necessary papers. Paul gave Tom a stern look. Tom glanced at his father and stared at the floor. As soon as everything was signed the custody sergeant told Tom to report to Gwynedd Magistrates Court on August 13. "If you fail to do so you'll be arrested and brought back here. Do you understand?"

"Yeah," said Tom, in feeble voice.

Mark nudged his client. "Yes, Sergeant."

"Yes, Sergeant," repeated Tom.

All three walked outside. Paul thanked his lawyer then watched him drive off. He looked at Tom. "Get in the car."

"Are we going back to Bryn Mawr?" asked Jessica hopefully, as Paul started the engine.

"No we're not going back to Bryn Mawr! We're going home!

"Why should *my* holiday be ruined? I didn't do anything."

Paul lost it. "Not another word, young lady. Understand?"

Jessica nodded meekly. "Yes, Dad."

Paul turned and glared at his son cowering in the back. "And you, Mr. Big-Time-Rich-Guy, wait till I get you home!"

Six

Tom stood trail at Gwynedd Magistrates Court, pleading guilty to common assault. Because of his age and previous good character he was issued with an £850 fine, which Paul duly paid. As punishment he was grounded for the rest of August. When he returned to school, instead of being treated like an outcast, as his mother predicted, his arrest and subsequent trial gave him celebrity status. Nervous and contrite at home, he was all of a swagger when he stepped through the school gates. Whereas Tom's reputation soared, Becky was branded a cheap whore who deserved everything she got. It wasn't long before Tom fell in with a group of notorious rich kids from Alderley Edge. With Jessica now studying at Bristol University and Tom staying out most nights of the week, Wren House felt empty. Sarah felt the emptiness the most. Paul was like a stranger, setting out early for the office and returning home late, tired and fit for nothing but eating dinner and falling asleep on the sofa.

Paul waited until after the trial to celebrate the upswing in company profits, whisking Sarah off to the Ritz Hotel in Paris for a long weekend. They stayed in the Windsor Suite, enjoying the best money could buy.

Careful not to make the same mistake he did in Dubai, Paul made sure ran everything past Sarah first.

"Fancy going to the Louvre this morning to see the Mona Lisa?"

Lying in bed Sarah could hear breakfast being laid in the next room, with its elegant mix of French and English furniture and views onto Place Vendôme. She was tired and hung over from the previous night. The last thing she wanted to do was traipse round an art gallery. Before flying to Paris she'd watched a documentary on Netflix about Marilyn Monroe, how she'd often kick-start her day with a Bloody Mary.

Maybe I should? No, absolutely not.

She stretched and sighed, "I feel like a lie-in."

"A lie-in! We're in Paris! You don't lie-in in Paris."

Sarah pulled the sheets over her head. "I do."

Paul stared at her inert body. He gave it a nudge. "Let's have breakfast and hit the streets."

"No."

"We could go up the Eiffel Tower?"

"I went up there years ago on a school trip."

"Doesn't matter… Come on."

"No."

"*Sarah!*"

"*No!* You go if you want."

Paul threw off the sheets. "Right!"

He took a shower, got dressed and breakfasted alone amidst the sumptuous furnishings and soft Parisian light. The table was loaded with goodies – croissants, fresh strawberries, slices of smoked bacon, scrambled eggs, figs, brioche – all laid out on a crisp white tablecloth. He picked up the silver coffee pot and poured the steaming liquid into a delicate china cup rimmed with gold. He took a sip and stared out onto Place Vendôme.

This is the life.

"Hey, Sarah. Would you like breakfast in bed? There's loads of food."

Silence... Paul got up and walked to the bedroom door, pressing his ear against the polished veneer; he could hear the faintest of snores coming from within. He inched opened the door and peeped inside. Sarah was lying on her back dead to the world, her mouth wide open.

Paris, city of love!

Car horns, the rush of tourists and locals, the shaded colonnades of the Rue de Castiglione. Paul headed towards the Tuileries past exclusive shops and restaurants. Turning right onto the Rue de Rivoli he made his way to Place de la Concorde. He wandered aimlessly across the square, stopping at the Egyptian obelisk. From base to tip he scanned the line of hieroglyphs covering its surface. What did they all mean? A mystery. His life was a mystery – his wife, his children, his marriage.

Hey, stop that. You're here to enjoy yourself.

In the distance he could see the Eiffel Tower rearing up.

It's alright her saying she's been up there before. I haven't.

He crossed Ponte de la Concorde, turned right onto Quai d'Orsay and followed the course of the Seine. Every now and then he came across courting couples wrapped in each other arms. Arriving at the Champs de Mars he joined a long line of tourists queuing at the foot of the Eiffel Tower. Half an hour later he got in the lift and was whisked to the top. The windblown view of Paris took his breath away. He imagined Sarah standing there as a schoolgirl. What was going through her mind? Looking down he retraced his journey back to her — through the Champ de Mars, along Quai d'Orsay, over Ponte de la Concord, past the obelisk, right on the Rue de Rivoli, left onto the Rue Castiglione, back to Place Vendome and their suite at the Ritz — back to day they first met. He was a lowly data inputer back then. Meeting her was the best thing that ever happened to him. From that day on he swore that, no matter what, he would work hard and make a success of his life.

☯

"You'll have to help me with this."

Paul was standing in front of the mirror in the main bedroom of Wren House. For the past ten minutes he'd been struggling with his cravat.

"Sarah!"

"Coming!"

Sarah walked in wearing a pink Chanel suit with gold buttons she'd bought in Paris. She took one look at him. "What you like!" She moved closer — "Come here" — took hold of the cravat and began to wrap it expertly around his neck.

"You look nice."

She smiled. "Thanks. You're not too bad yourself."

Beneath the aroma of Chanel No. 5 Paul caught

a whiff of alcohol.

She moved away quickly. "There you go."

It was late October and they were about to set off for Mike's wedding. Much to everyone's surprise the eternal bachelor was tying the knot. His bride was the beautiful blonde girl Paul had encountered on the night of Tom's 18th. Twenty years Mike's junior, Amy was your typical Cheshire girl — bold, brash, and full of confidence. After a whirlwind romance Mike had proposed in St. Lucia, presenting her with an 18-carat diamond ring on the beach at sunset. When he walked into Paul's office on his first day back at work and told him he was getting married Paul nearly fell off his chair.

"Shame Jess and Tom can't come to the wedding," said Paul, closing the front door and walking towards his pride and joy: his polished black Bentley GT. "Mike's almost their uncle."

Sarah opened the passenger door. "Probably too boring for them."

Paul got in, slipping on his seat belt. "What are they up to this weekend?"

Sarah climbed in sucking a Polo mint. "Jess is in London and Tom's gone to Amsterdam."

"Amsterdam? Since when?"

"Paul! He told you last week."

"Did he? I don't remember."

"We were having breakfast when he mentioned he was going. I was there!"

Paul didn't like his wife's insistent tone. "Alright, Sarah. Bloody hell. It obviously slipped my mind.

Been mad busy at work."

She wanted to say, 'Tell me something I don't know,' but didn't.

The wedding was taking place a few miles down the road at St. Peter's Church in Prestbury. All the way there Sarah kept fidgeting with the strap of her Rolex.

"What's the matter?" asked Paul.

"Nothing."

He gestured to her hands. "Look at you. You're a bag of nerves."

She stopped fiddling with her watch and placed her hands in her lap. There was an awkward silence. Paul hated silence. "Oh, I forgot to tell you. You should see the house Mike's just bought: big old Georgian place in Nether Alderley. Makes Wren House look like a shoebox…. Tell you what, Amy's not daft marrying Mike."

Sarah looked out of the passenger window. "Good luck to her." Paul gave her a double take.

Inside the church Sarah felt hot and clammy. As the organ played softly in the background and everyone waited for the bride, she stared over the heads of the packed congregation at the stained-glass window above the altar. The bright, sunlit colours began to melt, making her dizzy.

"Sarah!"

"Umm?"

"I said doesn't Mike's mum look well for her age?"

"Yes," she answered, without looking.

Suddenly the organ began to play 'The Wedding March'. Everyone stood and turned round. A smiling

Amy emerged into the church, walking up the aisle on the arm of her father. While the rest of the congregation admired her dress Paul couldn't take his eyes off Mike; he was transfixed by his bride-to-be, a look of utter devotion on his face. Mike whispered something to his Best Man — his brother Terry — who nodded and checked his inside pocket. Sarah watched the ghostly figure of Amy float up the aisle. Reaching the altar Mike took hold of her hand and gave it a reassuring squeeze. The vicar smiled at them both then invited the congregation to sit. After a long-winded talk about the sanctity of marriage Mike and Amy recited their vows.

"To have and to hold, from this day forward, for better, for worse, for richer, for poorer, in sickness and in health, to love and to cherish... "

Amused at Amy's enthusiastic 'for richer', Paul glanced at Sarah. He was about to make a joke when he noticed tears streaming down her face.

When the service was over everyone filed outside the church for the photographs. Watching Mike and Amy pose in the doorway Paul slipped his arm around Sarah's waist. "Not like you to get emotional at weddings?"

She shrugged, "Yeah well..." then looked at the photographer who was busily arranging yet another shot. "How long's this gonna take! *Bloody* hell!"

"Calm down, Sarah. What's the rush?"

The rush was for the rows of champagne flutes lined up inside the reception area at Capesthorne Hall. Mike had spared no expense booking one of the finest wedding venues in Cheshire, and Sarah wasted no time taking advantage of the hospitality. As soon as they arrived Paul watched her dash over, grab a glass of bubbly, gulp it down then picked up another two glasses and carried them back.

"I needed that," she sighed, handing him a glass. "It was hot inside that church. Didn't you think it was hot?"

Paul eyed her suspiciously. "Not really."

"I did." She took another sip, her mood rapidly improving. She scanned the hundred or so guests filling the room. "Good turnout… Gorgeous place… Ooh! Doesn't Tilly look nice in that dress? She's got a great figure, hasn't she?"

Paul was about to answer when Sarah marched over to Tilly, kissed her on both cheeks and motioned to her dress, nodding her approval. Sipping their drinks both women fell into animated conversation.

Paul felt a tap on his shoulder, "Alright, Paul?"

It was Terry; Mike's brother. "Hey, Terry. I'm looking forward to your speech."

"I'm not. I hate making speeches, hence…" he lifted a large glass of scotch.

"You'll be fine."

Terry moved closer and asked, in a half whisper, staring over at his brother's new wife, "What do you think of Amy?"

"Don't really know her. I've only met her the once, at Tom's 18th."

"Well err… I think she's a gold digger."

Paul glanced over at Amy; she was standing by the

French Windows bathed in sunlight, a huge grin on her face.

"Really?"

"Without a doubt. I mean, *look* at her. She's absolutely gorgeous." He gulped his scotch down in one. "Our Mike's a lot of things, but he's no Brad Pitt."

Paul laughed. "You're not wrong there." He caught sight of a beaming Mike talking to Amy's father. "Still, as long as he's happy."

"Yeah but for how long?"

"Give it a chance, Terry. Bloody hell. They've only just tied the knot."

"No, Paul. It's the same old story — beautiful girl marries plain-looking rich guy. Before you know it she's bored shitless and off doing all sorts. Cheshire's full of marriages like that. I read somewhere it's the divorce capital of the UK."

"Terry! Over here!"

It was Mike, waving at his brother. Terry patted Paul's arm. "Not a word to Mike."

"Course not. Good luck with the speech."

"Cheers, bud."

During the meal Sarah became more and more inebriated. Barely able to string two words together she picked at her desert, giggling as a piece of chocolate mousse fell off her spoon into her lap. Luckily the other guests seated around the table were too drunk to notice.

Paul noticed, hissing, "For God's sake, Sarah. Get a grip."

"Oh shut up... Misery guts." Smirking, she reached out towards her glass of red wine the waiter had just refilled.

Paul grabbed her wrist. "Don't you think you've had enough?"

"GET OFF!"

Paul instantly let go, embarrassed by the look of concern from the other guests. Sarah picked up her glass and gulped it down. She stared at Paul smugly, her watery eyes full of malice.

The DJ's voice came over the PA inviting the happy couple to take to the dance floor. Mike and Amy obliged, dancing awkwardly to Adele's 'When We Were Young.' As the spotlight picked them out everyone around the table smiled and nodded, Paul looked at Sarah; she was staring down into her half-eaten chocolate mousse, mumbling incoherently. After the applause died down the DJ cranked out 'Celebrate' by Kool and the Gang. Suddenly Tilly appeared at their table, placing her hands on Sarah's shoulders. "Come on, girl. Let's party!"

Energised, Sarah got to her feet and followed her friend onto the packed dance floor. Paul took a sip of red wine, watching as his wife cavorted with a group of equally drunk middle-aged women. Where were their husbands? Probably sitting on the sidelines like Paul.

It's the same old story – beautiful girl marries plain-looking rich guy. Before you know it she's bored shitless and off doing all sorts. Cheshire's full of marriages like that.

Paul congratulated himself that Sarah had fallen

in love with him before he made his fortune. It wasn't the case with Tilly, who at that moment was shaking her ample booty to Beyoncé's 'Crazy in Love'. She was married to Simon, a mega-wealthy accountant from Prestbury. Paul often came across him at the golf club. Short and fat with the face of a weasel. And arrogant with it, boasting to anyone who'd listen about the numerous homes he had around the globe.

"Paul! Paul!"

Tilly came rushing towards him in a panic.

"What's wrong?"

"It's Sarah. She's passed out in the loo!"

"Oh for…"

Paul got to his feet and followed Tilly into the ladies. A gurgling sound came from one of the cubicles. Tilly pushed open the door. Sarah was lying on her back, her pink Chanel suit covered in vomit.

"Shit!" Paul sat her up, resting her back against the toilet. "Sarah… Sarah." He tapped her face gently. "Sarah."

"Uggggggh…."

"Oh baby, what's happened?"

A string of saliva oozed from her mouth. "Pa-ul."

"That's right, it's Paul."

"Pa-ul." She tried lifting head but it kept falling to her chest.

Paul looked at Tilly in a panic. "I'm taking her to the hospital. Give me a hand."

They hoisted her up and carried her into the car park. While Paul dug into his pocket for the keys to his Bentley, Sarah was making yet more gurgling noises.

He opened the rear door and put her in the back. He thanked Tilly, jumped in and roared off. Driving along the dark country lanes he kept glancing in the rear-view mirror at Sarah, her inert body lolling from side to side.

"I'm taking you to the hospital, Sarah. Hang in there. You'll be alright."

"I'll-be-alright," she slurred. She kept repeating the phrase over and over again. Suddenly she threw up, vomit splattering the back seat.

Oh God!

The smell was awful. "Hang on Sarah, we're almost there."

Seven

"We've pumped your wife's stomach and given her a sedative. She'll be fine now," explained the doctor. "I have to say, she had a dangerous amount of alcohol in her system. Is she a heavy drinker?"

Standing at the nurses' station staring at his wife comatose in bed midway down the ward Paul was as mystified as the doctor. Was she a heavy drinker? She could be for all he knew. He had his suspicions — the smell of alcohol on her breath when he came home from work, her constant tiredness at the end of each day. But he put that down to her lifestyle. She was one of the Ladies who Lunch, and he was proud of that. Proud that his wife didn't have to worry about everyday concerns — bills, mortgage payments, the constant need to live within your means. It was one of the reasons he worked so hard.

"Not really. I mean, she *enjoys* a drink. Who doesn't? But I wouldn't say she was a 'heavy drinker', no."

"I see… So err, how much does your wife consume on a daily basis, in your estimation?"

A bottle of champagne? Two bottles of vodka? It could be anything. He was hardly at home to find out. Embarrassed he didn't know the answer, he lied, "Oh not much; a few glasses of wine in the evening. Like most people."

"Most people don't end up in hospital having their stomach pumped."

"True. True… But this is just a one-off. Honestly. Sarah's a sensible girl."

"I see," said the doctor, suspiciously. "Well I hope this will be a lesson to her. Far too many middle-aged women abuse alcohol these days. It's a growing trend, I'm afraid."

"When can she go home?"

"Tomorrow, probably. We'll keep her in for a couple of nights to make sure there are no complications."

"I'll come back later then. Thanks, doctor."

Paul left the hospital in a daze and walked to his car. As he got behind the wheel the smell of vomit hit him, making him gag. Despite it being a chilly autumn morning he lowered the electric roof and took a few deep breaths. He was dog-tired after a long night in A&E. He started the car and drove home. When he got there a strange thing happened. Instead of the usual happy sight that greeted him, he found the house desolate and forlorn. His spirits lifted when he saw Tom's Audi TT on the drive; then remember his son was in Amsterdam.

Just me, then.

He crunched over the gravel and parked opposite the front door. All the way home he'd been putting off the inevitable. He braced himself and glanced over his shoulder into the back.

Oh God

The contents of Sarah's stomach were splattered

across the seat. He took out his phone and rang a mobile car valeting company he often used.

"It's a bit of a mess Greg, sorry. Someone's thrown up in the back… OK, great. I'll leave the car unlocked as usual."

Paul opened the front door. The house was silent. He trudged upstairs and fell into bed.

He woke up a little after midday with a banging headache, his short sleep invaded by a terrible nightmare. He dreamt that Jessica had been kidnapped and he was driving down to Bristol with a suitcase full of cash. Throughout the journey her tortured screams kept coming over the radio, "Help me, Daddy! Please!" He listened to her anguished cries, smashing the steering wheel with his fist. He drove as fast as he could, but every few miles the motorway was gridlocked. By the time he got to Bristol it was dark. He pulled up in a remote spot in the woods, grabbed the suitcase and jumped out of the car. He shouted his daughter's name over and over again. Hearing a noise he spun round. Sarah was standing behind him wearing her vomit-soaked Chanel suit, a look of contempt on her face. She lifted her hand slowly and pointed at something on the ground. Paul approached the bundle nervously — it was Jessica's naked body, bruised, battered and scarred. He was too late to save her. He fell to his knees, sobbing uncontrollably.

Jess!

He slid his phone off the bedside table and called his daughter in Bristol. He was relieved to hear she was having lunch with some friends in a city-centre brasserie.

"Is everything alright, Dad? You sound stressed."

"No, no. I'm fine, Jess. Everything's fine."

"How was the wedding?"

"Oh we had a great time... When are you home next? Christmas, isn't it?"

"*Daad!* What ya like! I'm spending Christmas in Rome this year with Claudia's family. I *told* you."

"Did you?"

"Yes!"

"Oh. Sorry, Jess."

"I might pop back for the weekend before then. I'll see how it goes."

"OK... Miss you."

"Are you *sure* you're alright?"

"Yeah, yeah. You take care. Bye."

"Oh. How's Mum?"

"She's fine... Out shopping as usual."

Jessica laughed. "She knew what she was doing marrying you, Dad. Bye."

"Bye love."

Paul lay in bed gathering his thoughts. A feeling of emptiness swept over him. Eventually he got up and took a shower. As he was getting dressed he looked out of the window; Jack and Grace were on the fringes of the wood. Grace was carrying a wicker basket. They were walking slowly through the undergrowth, staring at the ground.

What are they doing?

Then Jack called Grace over to him. He bent down and removed something white from the ground.

Grace smiled joyfully and put it in the basket, planting a kiss on his cheek. It was a mushroom. They were gathering mushrooms. Paul burst into tears. He sat on the edge of the bed, his mind in turmoil.

What is it? What is it?

Desperate for an answer he rushed downstairs. He threw on his jacket and opened the back door. He walked into the ornamental garden, opened the little wooden gate and headed across the field. Taking his usual route through the woods he suddenly stopped next to a huge oak tree.

What am I doing? Go home... No.

He walked on until he came to the cottage, a wisp of smoke drifting up from the chimney. It all looked so peaceful. He stared at it for a moment, then, on autopilot, skirted the fence until he found himself outside the back door. A strong smell of garlic and the sound of voices. He inched his way to the window and peeped inside — Jack and Grace were sitting at the kitchen table about to eat a large plate of cooked mushrooms. While Grace poured the tea Jack cut two slices of bread. He spread a thick layer of butter over each slice then handed one to Grace. They looked at each other expectantly before tucking in.

Grace rolled her eyes. "Umm... I tell you what, love. It doesn't get much better than this."

Jack tore off part of the crust and dragged it across his plate, soaking up the juices. "You're right, Grace. Nothing like the taste of freshly picked mushrooms and homemade bread." He popped the crust into his mouth. "Umm. Heaven."

A trickle of butter oozed from his lips. Paul watched as Grace picked up a paper napkin, leaned across the table and dabbed the corner of his mouth.

"Thanks, love."

Paul felt something break inside him. Dizzy, he staggered back, knocking over a watering can. Jess started barking.

Shit!

He dashed around the side of the cottage, jumped over the fence and ran into the woods. Heart pounding he sprinted through a thick clump of ferns, not stopping until he reached the oak tree. He leaned against it, catching his breath. Suddenly it began pouring with rain. He took off his jacket and lifted his face to the sky.

Later that day Paul received a phone call from the hospital to say that Sarah was fit to go home.

"Really? Only the doctor told me you were keeping her in for another night?"

"That won't be necessary. She's fine, if a little groggy. You can pick her up anytime."

"Thanks, Sister. I'm on my way."

"Oh; she asked me to tell to you to bring a fresh set of clothes."

"Of course. See you in a bit."

He went upstairs to the main bedroom and opened Sarah's wardrobe. There were racks and racks of designer clothes, some he'd never seen. He picked out a beige polo neck sweater and a knee-length skirt. Sliding the skirt off its hanger it came away and fell to the bottom of the wardrobe. As he reached inside to pick it up he felt a circular glass object. He lifted it out: it was a half empty bottle of vodka. He went cold. His first thought was to flush it down the loo, but then Sarah would only realise he'd discovered her guilty secret. She probably felt embarrassed enough as it is without that. He decided to put it back and closed the door. Frightened of what else he might find he pulled open her underwear draw and grabbed the first matching pair of bra and panties he came across.

It was almost dark when he left the house. He walked towards his Bentley, pressing his key fob. The interior light came on. He looked in the back tentatively – both seats had been scrubbed, the carpet vacuumed, the leather interior gleaming. He got in and started her up. Despite Greg using a ton of air freshener the unmistakable smell of vomit lingered in the background. Paul knew he would never get rid of it, no matter how many times he had the car valeted. It would be there for all time; a memory of that awful night.

Sarah was sitting beside her bed when he arrived. Dressed in a hospital gown, her face devoid of makeup, she looked tired and vulnerable. Not wanting to embarrass her, he approached the bed in a light-hearted way.

"There she is. All set?"

"Did you bring my clothes?" she asked, her eyes fixed to the floor.

Paul put the bag onto the bed. "Sure did."

She got up and closed the curtain between them.

"Won't be a minute."

Paul was sure the old lady in the bed opposite had detected malice in Sarah's voice. He smiled at her as he continued his banal chitchat through the curtains. "I brought you a nice warm jumper. It's cold outside."

The lady opposite smiled. "Chilly, is it?"

"Yes," answered Paul, glad of someone to talk to seeing as his wife was ignoring him. "Winter's on its way."

"I'm dreading it. It's so expensive to heat the house these days. I don't know how I'm going to manage."

Something Sarah doesn't have to worry about.

"I bet… Do you live locally?"

"I do, love. Wythenshawe born and bred. Where do you live?"

"Alderley Edge."

"Ooh! *Very* posh."

Paul revelled in the glamour. "Yeah, we love it—"

Sarah swished back the curtain. "Right let's go," and walked past him.

The old lady gave Paul a sympathetic look. "Bye, love."

Driving back from the hospital Paul continued the small talk in the hope of drawing a line under yesterday's embarrassing events. "I spoke to Jess earlier. She was out in Bristol having lunch with her friends. She's gonna try and make it home before Christmas... That'll be nice, eh?"

He glanced at Sarah; she was staring out of the window, lost in thought. As the heater kicked in the faint smell of vomit rose in the air.

Sarah blinked. "You got the car cleaned then?"

"Sure did," said Paul, upbeat. "No problem. Greg came over. Did it in no time."

Sarah gave a slight nod then stared longingly at the welcoming lights of a passing country pub. Paul noticed. In the past he would have suggested going for a drink. Not tonight.

She sensed his hesitancy. She let out a sigh and lapsed into silence. When they got home she traipsed into the lounge and sat on the sofa.

Paul closed the curtains. "That's it, you relax. Tea?"

"No thanks." She picked up a magazine then put it down. "Did you tell Jess what happened?"

"No. Why would I? It was just one of those things."

Sarah mulled this over, repeating to herself. "Just one of those things… Right."

Paul was desperate to change the subject. "I've just noticed. Where's your suit?"

"My suit?"

"Your Chanel suit you wore at the wedding."

"Oh, I gave it to one of the nurses."

"You did what! Cost a fortune that!" As soon as he spoke he knew he'd said the wrong thing.

Sarah glared at him "It was covered in vomit, Paul!"

Again he couldn't help himself. "You could have got it cleaned."

"What? Like the car, you mean? I could smell sick the moment I got in."

"Well I'd better get rid of it then!"

She jumped up. "Oh do what you want. You always have done."

"What's *that* supposed to mean?"

She walked to the door.

"Sarah?"

She opened it —Good night!" she shouted —slamming it shut.

Eight

While Paul's business flourished, the run-up to Christmas masked the slow disintegration of his marriage. Problems were buried beneath an avalanche of to-do lists, present-buying and pre-Christmas parties.

Six weeks had passed since Mike's wedding. Instead of cutting down on alcohol Sarah seemed to be drinking more. The moment he got home from work she opened a bottle of wine and poured two glasses, handing him one with a smirk. Paul was sure she did this to mask the lingering smell of booze from her lunchtime drinking. Conversation was stilted…

"How was work?"

"Busy. How was your day?"

"Fine. Had lunch with the girls."

Whenever they went out for a meal, which happened less and less these days, Paul had to wait until the first glass of wine kicked in before Sarah showed any sign of affection. The old Sarah. The one he fell in love with. Sitting opposite her, watching as she became steadily inebriated, he thought about the half-empty bottle of vodka he'd discovered at the bottom of her wardrobe. The house was full of booze, so why she had to hide it was beyond him. Since that awful night at the hospital he'd never once brought the subject up. He did this for two reasons. Firstly, he didn't want to embarrass her, and secondly, the surest way to propel someone towards alcohol is to warn them against it. Reverse psychology, according to an article he'd read by an expert who understood the inner workings of an addict's mind. But as far as Paul could see his ingenious strategy was having the opposite effect. Why in God's name did she drink so much? She never used to. And it was the worst time of the year to do anything about it. The world and his wife drink too much on the lead-up to Christmas, which, in Paul's eyes, arrived earlier and earlier each year. Everywhere you went people were drinking. You couldn't step out of the door without someone shoving a glass in your hand! So to even suggest cutting down would mark him out as miserable sod, a party-pooper who didn't have a happy bone in his body. He realised that the festive season is tailor-made for alcoholics – it allows them to hide in plain sight.

During the second week of December Paul and Mike flew to Madrid on a three-day business trip. Things had been so busy at work Paul hadn't had time to ask Mike about married life. He was eager to find out what the eternal bachelor made of it. On the flight over he got his answer.

"Should have done it years ago, mate. Just to wake up every morning next to Amy is a dream come true."

"Settled into your new house?"

"Oh yeah. Amy loves it. She's like the lady of the manor."

"Does she mind you going away this close to Christmas?"

Mike smirked, "Not when I promised to bring her back a mink coat. That's as well as her Christmas present."

"What have you bought her?"

"Oh I've spoilt her, mate. I mean, *seriously.* Her main present is a Bentley GT; like yours, only in blue. Can't wait to see her face on Christmas morning… What've you bought Sarah?"

"Nothing yet."

"I hear Madrid's got some fabulous jewellers."

"Sarah's got loads of jewellery."

"What about a car?"

"I bought her a brand new Merc when we came back from Paris."

"Designer dress?"

"Her wardrobe's full of them."

Mike buckled up before landing. "You'll think of something."

The outcome of the trip was a foregone conclusion; the Spanish civil engineering giant had made it plain they were eager to switch to InovaSystems payroll software. As soon as Paul and Mike landed they rolled out the red carpet, booking them into one the swankiest hotel in Madrid: the five-star Mandarin Oriental. The deal was signed the next day. To celebrate, the CEO, Señor Pablo Ruiz, treated Paul and Mike to dinner at the three Michelin-star DiverXO. As each delicious course was laid out in front of him Mike took a photo and sent it to Amy. He was like a lovesick teenager. Almost immediately his phone pinged a reply. Mike showed Paul one of Amy's cute messages – four throbbing hearts and a 'So miss you babes xxx'. Paul decided to send Sarah a photo of his dessert. He waited for a reply… His phoned remained silent.

The next morning, with business concluded earlier than expected, Paul and Mike had a free day to do as they pleased. Mike had promised to buy Amy a fur coat while Paul was keen to get Sarah a Christmas present. So on the advice of the hotel concierge they took a taxi to Calle Gran Via, Madrid's most exclusive shopping district. When they got there they split up and arranged to meet back at the hotel for lunch.

Paul wandered round in a daze, popping into various designer boutiques — Dior, Versace, Chanel, Hermés — surveying the endless racks of clothes, shoes and handbags. But all this did was confuse him. What would she like? He thought about ringing her to ask. He quickly discounted that. Not much thought there. He had all the money in the world yet had no idea what to buy his wife. In the end he plumped for the most expensive thing he could find – a Birkin Bag at 69,000 Euros.

When he got back to the hotel Mike couldn't wait to show Paul Amy's fur coat. He opened the wardrobe with a flourish. "Take a look at this!" and brought out an ankle-length mink, twisting it on its hanger. "Stunning eh? It's the real thing. None of your faux fur for my Amy."

"Very nice."

Mike noticed Paul was carrying a Hermés

shopping bag. "You managed to find something for Sarah then?"

"Yeah. I really pushed the boat out. Cost sixty K. Hope she likes it." He removed the handbag. "What do you think?"

Mike gave him the thumbs up. "Oh she'll love it, mate! What woman wouldn't, at that price." He picked it up, examining it closely. "Mind you, how they've got the nerve to charge sixty grand for this is unbelievable. Looks like any other bag to me."

Paul was quick to jump to his own defence. "That's what I thought. But according to the woman at the shop it's the most coveted handbag on the planet. All the A-listers have got one. She said it's a fashion icon. Women go mad for them, evidently."

"Really?" Mike grabbed his phone. "Hold on." He took a photo. "I'll send it to Amy. She knows all about fashion. Let's see what she thinks."

A few seconds later Mike's phone pinged. He read the message. "Bloody hell, you're not wrong. Listen to this. 'OMG! I would kill for a Birkin!' There's your answer, mate." Mike put the bag down and pondered. "Should have bought Amy one."

"You've spent enough on her already."

"True, true… I'll get her one for her birthday."

To celebrate the end of a successful year Paul and Mike gave each of their employees — a workforce that had grown to over thirty — a thousand pound bonus, which they handed out in cash on Christmas Eve. Everyone's faces lit up. At lunchtime boxes of pizza were delivered. Around 2 p.m. Paul wished his staff a Merry Christmas and told them they could go home. Mike was the first to leave. Paul had never seen him so excited; he obviously couldn't wait to get home and spend his first Christmas with his new wife. Paul remembered feeling exactly the same way. But that was in the past. Climbing into his Bentley he secretly dreaded what the next few days would bring.

Pulling up outside Wren House he was relieved to see a Christmas tree twinkling in the lounge window; a late addition to their usual raft of decorations. Sarah had obviously been busy. The festive sight settled his nerves. He got out of his car and walked towards the front door.

Orr, that's nice...

A Christmas wreath interlaced with holly had been attached to the brass knocker. Smiling, he looked up look the sky.

All we need now is for it to snow.

He opened the front door. "Hi!" and heard laughter coming from the lounge. He walked in to find Sarah and Tom sitting on the sofa sharing a bottle of wine. He glanced at Sarah; she didn't seem too drunk. For once.

"Hi, Dad."

"Tom! Great to see you... Hey, *The Great Escape* is on tonight if you fancy it?"

"Love to Dad but I'm going to a party at a mate's."

"Who?"

"You don't know him."

"I don't know any of your friends these days."

Tom shrugged.

"You'll be around for Christmas dinner tomorrow though won't you?"

"Of course he will," said Sarah. She put her arms around Tom's shoulders and gave him a hug. "You wouldn't miss it for the world, would you darling?"

"No, Mum."

"No. He's still my little boy."

Paul noticed his son cringe. He was strangely on edge, his eyes darting around the room. "Fancy a beer, Tom?"

"Sure."

Paul headed for the door.

Sarah shouted after him. "And bring another bottle of wine, babe. This one's almost finished."

Walking into the kitchen Paul felt his blood pressure rising. He opened the fridge, grabbed two beers and fizzed one open. He gulped most of it down then slid a bottle of Barolo from the wine rack.

"Ooh!" exclaimed Sarah, when Paul reappeared with the drinks. "Let's get this party started."

He handed his son a beer. "Here you go, Tom."

"Cheers." He sniffed, his nose twitching.

"Coming down with cold?"

Tom stared at the floor. "Not really... Might be... Anyway, Merry Christmas everyone!"

"Merry Christmas, darling!" Sarah emptied her glass then waved it at Paul, motioning him to the fresh bottle he'd placed on the coffee table. Paul fumed inside. He put on a false smile and opened the Barolo, filling her glass half way.

"Hey, Scrooge. Fill it up."

"Come on, Dad. It's Christmas."

Reluctantly Paul topped it up.

Sarah took a sip. As the alcohol seeped into her system she looked at the roaring log fire and fairy lights strung across the mantelpiece. "It's a shame Jess can't be here." She glanced at Paul, her eyes glazing over. "Orr, do you remember our first Christmas together?"

"Here we go," laughed Tom.

"No, no. Listen. It was before you were born… You're Dad and I had just got married. We were living in a tiny flat in Handforth. Do you remember Paul?"

Paul sipped his beer through gritted teeth. "I do, yeah."

"Above a launderette it was Tom. A real noisy place. We had no money back then. Your grandma had to pay for a taxi so we could go to hers for Christmas dinner."

"We weren't *that* broke," said Paul.

"We *were!*" She tipped back her wine. "Anyway, on Christmas morning Tom — I'll never forget this — your dad brings me breakfast in bed."

"You old romantic!"

"Wait, I've not finished yet. So I wake up and your dad's stood there with a tray of tea and toast, and he places it in my lap. On the tray was a red rose and small box done up in a bow."

"Orr, Dad!"

Paul began to blush.

"So I opened it and… and it was a small bottle of perfume… It… it didn't cost much, but…" Sarah's eyes filled with tears.

"What's wrong Mum?"

Paul jumped up. "Another beer, Tom?"

"Yeah, sure."

Paul picked up the bottle of Barolo. "Top-up, Sarah?"

Sarah got to her feet. "No thanks. She headed towards the door. "I… I need the loo."

When Sarah had left the room Tom gave Paul a concerned look. "What's wrong with Mum? I came home at lunchtime and she was still in her dressing gown. I had to put the rest of the decorations up. She just sat there staring into space… And why is she drinking so much? She never used to."

Paul sighed. "I don't know, Tom."

"You're not getting divorced are you?"

Paul saw genuine fear in his son's eyes."Of course not."

"Things aren't right though, are they? And don't pretend they are."

"We're just going through a rough patch, that's all. We'll work it out."

"I hope so. The last thing I want is you two splitting up. Half my mate's parents are divorced. What is it about round here?"

Paul sat next to Tom, placing a comforting hand on his knee. "We're not getting divorced, Tom."

"Promise?"

"Promise… Your mother she… she gets emotional

at Christmas. And Jess being in Rome hasn't helped. It'll be the first time we won't be together as a family." He tried to lighten the situation, nudging Tom in the ribs. "You know what mothers are like."

"Suppose." He finished his beer and got up. "Right. Better get a move on. I said I'd go round to Johnny's before heading to the party."

"OK. Have a nice time. See you tomorrow."

"Bye Dad… Enjoy the film."

Nine

Paul opened the curtains onto a cold, damp, Christmas morning. *No sign of snow. Ah well…* Everything was silent except for a crow cawing somewhere off in the woods. He glanced across the field towards the tree-line shrouded in mist at this early hour. About to step from the window he caught sight of a ghostly figure emerging from the mist. It was Jack; he was carrying a box of some sort. Paul watched as he made his way across the field and opened the little wooden gate. *Not now, Jack. Please.* Jack looked up. Noticing Paul standing in the window dressed in his pyjamas he gave him a wave and pointed to the back door. Jack disappeared under the eaves then reappeared moments later without the box, motioning to Paul he'd left something outside the back door.

Suddenly Paul understood. He smiled and waved, mouthing.

Thanks!'

Touched by his neighbour's thoughtfulness he watched him trek back across the field before vanishing into the mist. He slipped his dressing gown on and made his way downstairs, leaving Sarah fast asleep in bed. He walked into the kitchen and opened the back door. Lying on the step was a small box wrapped in Christmas paper tied with a red bow. He picked it up, closed the door and carried it to the marble worktop.

He undid the bow and tore open the lid. Nestling on top of white tissue paper was a handmade Christmas card — a watercolour of Wren House— inscribed 'To Paul, Sarah, Tom and Jessica. Merry Christmas, from Jack, Grace and Jess.' Paul delved into the box and brought out four pairs of woollen mittens, each pair differing in colour and knitted in quaint, naïve patterns. He held them in his hand, feeling their softness. He imagined Grace sitting by the fire night after night straining her eyes. He was lost for words. This kind, simple gesture gave him an idea. He switched the radio on and began to prepare breakfast.

"Merry Christmas!"

Sarah woke up to find Paul standing beside the bed holding a tray, a carrier bag looped in the crook of his left arm.

"Oh." She sat up, rubbing her eyes.

Paul placed the tray in her lap; it was a mirror-image of their first Christmas Day breakfast all those years ago — tea, toast and marmalade — except for the imitation red rose he'd borrowed from a vase in the hall. Back then it was the real thing.

Deeply touched, Sarah lowered her eyes. "Thank you."

"Ta *darrr!*" Paul placed the designer carrier-bag on the bed. "Merry Christmas, Sarah." He bent down and kissed her on the cheek; their first kiss in months. "Hope you like it."

Sarah read the word 'Hermés'. Her heart sank. But Paul was so excited she felt the need to offer a smile. "Ooh. What's this?"

"Open it and find out."

To give her more room he picked up the breakfast tray and placed it onto the bedside table. Grinning, he sat next to her on the bed. "I got it in Madrid. You do *not* want to know how much it cost."

Sarah steadied herself. She reached inside and pulled out the pink crocodile-skin Birkin Bag. She stared at the luxurious fashion icon, its classic shape famous the world over. She knew how much it had cost — Tilly had one, three in fact, bought by a doting husband. She closed her eyes. Paul took this for a show of emotion. He squeezed her hand. "Only the best for my Sarah."

She felt as if she was falling into a black hole. She needed to climb out, and fast. She opened her eyes and looked at the clock. "Is that the time!" She jumped out of bed, sending the Birkin Bag tumbling to the floor "I need to put the goose in the oven."

"Aren't you going to eat your breakfast?"

"Later. I'm not hungry."

Paul watched as she grabbed her dressing gown and hurried out. Desperate to start the day on a happy note he followed her down the stairs. "Jack came by this morning, at the crack of dawn."

"Oh yes?"

"Yeah. Dropped our present off. You should see what it is."

Sarah walked into the kitchen and spotted the open box on the worktop. While Paul removed the organic goose from the fridge she read the handmade card.

"It's Wren House!" Then she noticed the four pairs of mittens. She picked them up, examining each one carefully. She saw how different they all were, and how much work had gone into them. "How…how thoughtful." Her voice caught in her throat. "They're so love…"

Paul looked up. Tears were falling down his wife's face. He left the goose and hurried over, taking her in his arms. "Hey, what's all this? Don't cry." Out of his depth he attempted a joke. "If you don't like the bag I can always take it back."

She pulled away and ran out of the kitchen.

"Sarah! Tom'll be here soon!"

She dashed into the bedroom and made straight for the dressing table, yanking open the bottom drawer. She reached inside and removed her secret stash of Prozac. Trembling, she swallowed two tablets, went to the wardrobe and took out the vodka. She sat on the bed, glugging down four mouthfuls. Gradually, as the mixture of booze and medication kicked in, she began to see things differently. Why get upset over some silly gloves, running out of the kitchen like that? She noticed the Birkin Bag lying on the floor. She picked it up and caressed the ribbed crocodile skin, its pink glossy sheen. Countless times she'd seen the very same bag on the arm of an A-lister. She undid the gold clasp, opened the bag and put her nose inside, inhaling deeply — ah, the unmistakable smell of luxury. She really was a lucky woman. Lucky to have a husband like Paul who had brought her to this mansion and treated her like a queen, taking her to glamorous places, buying her the best of everything. What the hell was wrong with her? She was ungrateful. That's right. She was an ungrateful cow who didn't know how fortunate she was. She needed to behave like a proper loving wife.

She took a shower, put her makeup on then chose one of her designer dresses – a shimmering, low-cut Versace that Paul had bought her in Milan. She checked herself in the mirror, reached under the bed and took out Paul's present. Feeling calm and in control she went downstairs into the kitchen to find Paul staring nonplussed at the goose.

"It won't cook itself."

Paul turned to see Sarah standing behind him smiling. What a transformation.

She handed him his present. "Merry Christmas."

"Thanks!" He tore off the wrapping paper – it was a biography of Elon Musk.

Must have cost all of thirty quid. If that.

Now it was Paul's turn to feign enthusiasm. "Oh, great… Elon Musk."

"You said you liked him. Give you something to read on your next business trip."

He imagined the avalanche of expensive presents Amy must be showering on Mike at that very moment. "Yeah, yeah, sure." He kissed her on the cheek. "Thanks, Sarah."

She glanced at the goose. "Right! Let's get this thing in the oven."

As she pulled away he smelt the tell-tale reek of booze on her breath. He pictured her taking the vodka out of the wardrobe and swigging it down. Were things *really* that bad between them? It was Christmas Day for heaven's sake! He'd just given her the handbag of her dreams. Why did she feel the need to drink?

"Do you want me to do anything?"

"Open a bottle of white," she said, pulling out the giblets.

Should he? Yes he should. "Bit early for a drink."

"It's for the goose, Paul. I'm putting some in the roasting dish to add flavour."

He wanted the ground to open up. "Oh… right… Sorry."

"Mind you, it *is* Christmas... Tell you what, open a bottle of Sancerre: my favourite."

Paul was damned if he did and damned if he didn't. He really wanted the day to go well, so why not give it a rest and join his wife in a glass of wine? Where's the harm in that? It was Christmas after all. And thousands of couples in Cheshire were no doubt doing the same. Deep down he knew it was wrong, but to have the old Sarah back, even for one day, even an inebriated Sarah, would be worth the hassle.

Go on, push the boat out.

"Tell you what, babe. Sod the Sancerre. Let's have some champagne."

"Now you're talking! And turn the radio up."

Fuelled by vintage champagne and slushy Christmas songs the morning flew by. While Paul peeled the veg and laid the table, Sarah dressed the goose and prepared the starter. Paul cracked silly jokes, doing rude mimes with a parsnip. The more

Sarah drank the funnier he became. They hadn't got on this well in a long time.

When 'Last Christmas' by Wham came on the radio Sarah stopped what she was doing, her glassy eyes staring into the past "Do you remember this, babe? The night we first met? They played it at Michelle's party. Remember?"

He didn't. "Course I do."

"You asked me to dance and we had our first kiss."

She closed her eyes and began to sway. "Last Christmas I gave you my heart, the very next day you gave it away."

Paul put his knife down and took her in his arms. "This year, to save me from tears, I'll give it to someone special."

Sarah opened her eyes and stared into his. She closed them again, resting her head on his shoulder. They held each other tight, drifting slowly around the kitchen. Paul slid his hands down her back, squeezing her bottom. Sarah responded by pushing her hips gently into his groin. She found his mouth and they began to kiss passionately.

They were back in 1984, two young lovers about to embark on a new life.

"Take me to bed," she whispered.

They rushed up the stairs, crashed into the bedroom and got undressed. Paul had never felt so alive. His wife was coming back to him. Throwing her naked onto the bed he knelt down and parted her legs, kissing the inside of her thighs, biting them sharply. She groaned. Paul licked his way upwards, feasting on her salty core.

"Paul… *Paul…*"

Months without sex had caged his libido. Now it was free. He stood up and rolled her onto her stomach roughly. Once again Sarah groaned, louder this time. It was the sign he'd been waiting for. He climbed onto the bed, parted the cheeks of her bottom and began pounding away, each aggressive thrust sending shockwaves though her body.

"Paul!"

He leant down, biting her shoulder "You love it."

He carried on thrusting, thrilled at her rippling flesh.

He was imagining it, surely? No he wasn't. He eased down. Sarah was whimpering. He looked at her profile on the pillow. Tears were rolling down her cheek. She burst out crying, curling into a ball and sobbing. He lay next to her and gave her a cuddle.

"Sarah? What's wrong?"

"GET OFF!"

She jumped up, ran into the bathroom and locked the door.

Shit. Shit!

He went to the door. "Sarah? What's wrong?"

"You bastard!"

"I'm… I'm sorry. I thought you were into it."

"Leave me alone!"

"I said I'm sorry."

"Go away!"

He began to panic. "Tom'll be here soon… It… it's Christmas… Don't spoil it… Plea..."

Sarah yanked open the door wrapped in a towel. Sobbing, she brushed past him and snatched up her clothes. "Don't you *ever* do that to me again!"

"I said I'm sorry."

"Sorry? So you knew what you were doing then?"

Before he had chance to speak she rushed back into the bathroom and slammed the door.

Paul stood there in a state of shock, the euphoria of the morning replaced by a gathering headache. Then, suddenly, "Merry Christmas!" broke the silence. He went to the bathroom door, whispering frantically, "Tom's here!"

"Well go down and see him then!" came her exasperated reply.

Paul was scared to leave Sarah on her own in case she started on the vodka. But what could he do? He heard Tom coming up the stairs. "I'll be down in a minute, Tom. I've just had a shower."

"Where's Mum?"

Shit!

"She's in the shower. Go down and help yourself to a drink."

"OK."

Tom grinned as he headed down the stairs; he'd caught his parents having sex; that was obvious. Maybe they'd put their problems behind them? He hoped so.

Paul quickly got dressed and hurried downstairs. He composed himself and walked into the kitchen just as Tom was pulling a cold Becks from the fridge.

"Merry Christmas, Tom."

"Merry Christmas, Dad." He motioned to the stack of green bottles lying on the bottom shelf. "Want one?"

"No thanks… Oh go on then… Good night last night?"

Tom's eyes sparkled as he handed his dad a beer. "Yeah, we had a right laugh. Nick got absolutely wasted. Oh Dad it was so funny. He runs outside, right — this is about two o'clock in the morning — and jumps into the swimming pool. We couldn't believe it. His parents turn the heater off in winter yeah, so the water must have been *freezing*!"

"Bloody hell, dangerous that."

"He was that far gone he didn't even notice."

Paul smiled at Nick's antics. He was glad his son had enjoyed himself, yet suspicious of his rapid-fire, over-excited delivery.

"Sounds like one hell of a party."

"Wicked, yeah," he sniffled.

The kitchen door opened. "Who's wicked?"

Tom rushed to his mother and gave her a hug. "Merry Christmas, Mum. I was just telling Dad about Nick's party."

Sarah had changed into jeans and a pink cashmere sweater, her hair tied in a ponytail. Paul noticed how expertly she had applied her makeup – *viola:* a happy, prosperous housewife all set for Christmas Day. The image of her lying on the pillow sobbing came into his head. He felt ashamed.

Tom noticed. "What's wrong, Dad?"

Paul snapped out of it. "Nothing. Nothing. Just

thinking about Nick jumping into that freezing water."

"What's this?" asked Sarah.

Before Tom could answer the phone rang in the kitchen. He picked it up. "Mad house... Hi Jess! Merry Christmas!... Yeah, yeah. Just arrived… Yeah I'm here with them now… Mum, Jess wants a word… I'll just put her on… How's Rome by the way?.. Wow. Lucky bitch."

Sarah took the phone. "Don't call your sister that… Hi, darling. Merry Christmas…"

Paul felt like an outcast — the joyous look on Tom's face when his mother walked into the kitchen, the eagerness of him rushing to her; the fact that Jess wanted to speak Sarah and not him; the way Tom stayed close to his mother as she spoke on the phone – signs he was gradually becoming a stranger to his family.

What happened next proved it.

"…take care, Jess. Enjoy the rest of your holiday… Bye, darling."

Sarah hung up.

Paul was mortified. "Why didn't you pass me over?"

A glow of satisfaction dawned on Sarah's face. "Her friend was calling her. Apparently they're going out for lunch… Sorry."

"I wanted to speak to her."

"Never mind." She saw the hurt in Paul's eyes. "Call her back if you like?"

He shook his head. "Doesn't matter."

Sarah clapped her hands. "Right! Prezzy time!"

"Brilliant!" said Sam, downing his beer. He opened the fridge and pulled out another. "Want one, Dad?"

"No, thanks. I've not finished this one y..."

"I will!" Sarah picked up her glass and headed for the lounge. "Open another bottle of champagne would you, Paul."

Sarah and Tom left the kitchen. Annoyed at being treated like a servant, Paul realised he had penance to serve for what took place in the bedroom this morning. He couldn't believe how aggressive he was.

Where did that come from?

Mystified, he grabbed another bottle of champagne and walked into the lounge to see Tom throw his arms around Sarah.

"A Tag Heure! Oh Mum! Just what I wanted!" Deep down he was peeved it wasn't a Rolex, like Nick's. Ah well, maybe next year.

"Glad you like it," said Paul.

"Oh, yeah. Cheers Dad."

Tom strapped the watch to his wrist, examining it from all angles. "Nice."

"Suits you," said Sarah. "Not too showy."

"I like showy... Only joking, Mum. It's great."

In his eagerness to join in Paul put the cherry on the cake. "And err, I've... *We've* put some cash in the bank for you."

Tom's eyes lit up. "Brilliant!"

"Don't go spending it on useless stuff," warned Sarah. "It's for when you go to university next year."

"Course not, Mum." But already Tom was

thinking about the trip to Thailand the gang were planning in March. He could afford to go now. Get in. "What did Dad buy you?"

"Oh, a handbag," she answered, matter-of-fact."

"Nice… What did Mum get you, Dad?"

Sixty fucking grand I spent on that 'Oh, a handbag'. Ungrateful cow.

"Biography of Elon Musk."

"A book! Bloody hell, Mum, spoil him why don't you."

Desperate to get back in Sarah's good books Paul enthused, "No, it's exactly what I wanted… Can't wait to read..."

"It's got nothing to do with how much something costs, Tom," said Sarah, cutting across him.

Tom must have read his father's mind. "Yeah but it helps."

Sarah noticed the faintest of smiles appear on Paul's face. "No! Money's not everything! It's the thought that counts." She went to the Christmas tree and picked up the box Jack had kindly left outside the back door this morning. She removed the four pairs of woollen mittens, showing them to Tom. "Look what Jack and Grace gave us." She handed a pair to her son. "These are for you."

Amused, Tom turned them over in his hand. "Gloves. Whoopee do."

Sarah snapped. "Don't be so ungrateful! Look at the amount of work that's gone into them! Look! Hours and hours and hours."

"Alright, Mum. Bloody hell."

Then, more to Paul than to Tom, she said, "You can stuff your expensive presents. I'd rather have these anytime."

Paul's world was falling apart, right there in front of the twinkling Christmas tree and roaring log fire.

"That's told me," laughed Tom, breaking the silence. "Come on, Dad. What are you waiting for? Open the champagne."

"I thought you were on beer," was all Paul could bring himself to say.

"I'll have both... Come on Dad. It's Christmas."

"That's right, darling," said Sarah, holding out her glass with a cold, cynical smirk. "It's Christmas."

The dining room was a picture of Christmas cheer when they all sat down to eat, tipsy from a morning's drinking. Although the table groaned with goodies from the finest Cheshire delicatessens – an organic goose being the centrepiece – Tom and Sarah hardly touched their food. Sarah was more interested in the bottle of Grand Cru St. Emilion a client had given Paul, while Tom picked and sniffed at his meal.

"Come on, Tom. Eat up." encouraged Paul.

"I'm not that hungry." Tom got up for the third time during the meal. "Need the loo."

"Again!" said Paul. "And that cold of yours is getting worse."

When Tom left the room Paul looked at Sarah who was busy refilling her glass.

"What?" she slurred.

"I'm sorry."

She took a sip and stared at him. "For what,

exactly? For being an arsehole?"

"Don't say that."

"'Don't say that!" A trickle of red wine oozed from the corner of her mouth.

"You know what I mean. For this morning."

"Oh that?" she slurred, flinging him a contemptuous look. "Treating me like a piece of meat?" She nodded, "I see. That's alright then."

Paul handed his wife serviette, "You're dribbling."

She snatched it off him and threw it in his face.

Paul shot out of his seat. "I'm not putting up with this. I've really tried today."

"Oh he's really tried today. Oh thank you, Paul. Thank you *so* much for trying."

"There's no talking to you, is there?"

She gave a drunken shrug. "Nope."

"Right." He pulled open the door and left the room, slamming it behind him.

As he was climbing the stairs he heard Sarah give an exasperated scream followed by the sound of breaking glass. He rushed back across the hall and opened the door. Sarah was slumped in the chair with a smug look on her face, the £400 bottle of wine smashed against the fireplace.

"That's right, Sarah. Wreck the place."

She picked up her wineglass and hurled it at him. Paul closed the door just in time to hear it smash. He rushed up the stairs and walked down the landing towards the sanctuary of his bedroom. The opening bars of a thrash metal track came booming from Tom's room.

For God's sake!

Paul was about to give him what for when he looked through a gap in the door and saw Tom leaning over a vanity mirror snorting a line of coke. He fell back against the wall — his wife was drinking herself to death and now his son was taking hard drugs. To escape the madness he rushed downstairs and flung open the front door. With no idea where he was going he ran down the drive, clambered over a stile and made his way into the woods, not stopping until he reached the large oak tree. He leaned against it to catch his breath. Suddenly it began to snow. He paced up and down, his mind in turmoil. Emotionally and physically drained, his legs gave way and he slumped down against the base of a tree. He thought about the wonderful Christmas Mike and Amy must be having, comparing it to the disastrous one unfolding at Wren House. Unable to suppress his emotions he put his head between his knees and began to sob. None of this was part of the glamorous future he'd envisioned for his family at the start of his business career. Why had it turned out like this? He'd worked all the hours God sent, done everything he could for his family, only to be sat in the middle of a freezing cold forest sobbing his heart out.

Suddenly the distant sound of Tom's voice. *"DAD!... DAD!"*

Paul instinctively knew something was wrong. He got up and sprinted as fast as he could through the snow. Jumping over the stile he ran up the drive. A distraught Tom was standing outside the front door.

"Dad!… It's… it's Mum. She's..."

"What's happened?"

"I... I can't wake her up!"

"What? Where is she?"

"In her bedroom."

They rushed inside, up the stairs and down the landing. Bursting into the bedroom they found Sarah lying on the bed next to a bottle of vodka and an empty strip of prescription pills.

"Oh God, no. Sarah!"

Paul sat her up, slapping her face. "Sarah... Sarah…" Panicking, he looked at Tom. "Phone an ambulance."

Scared out of his wits Tom just stared at the floor.

"TOM! PHONE AN AMBULANCE!"

Ten

There it was. The house of their dreams; a detached Victorian red brick villa set in ten acres of Cheshire countryside.

"Oh my God!" exclaimed Jyoti. "Look at it! It's perfect!"

"Amazing darling."

"Let's buy it."

"Hold on a minute. We've not seen inside yet."

"So what. We can always redecorate." She grabbed his hand. "This is the place, Sanjeev. I can feel it."

Jyoti's impulsiveness worried the hell out of Sanjeev; they had been married for less than a year and already she was spending money like water; cars, clothes, holidays and now this. He only had himself to blame. As heir to the Ahmed clothing fortune Sanjeev had been raised by doting parents who had given him the best of everything. So when he first set eyes on the shy, working-class beauty who worked in the company's IT department, he set about wooing her the only way he knew how – by sweeping her off her feet and spoiling her. It was, after all, the way his father had won his mother, and kept her by his side all these years. How else was a chubby, balding twenty-five-year-old going to win the heart of such a beautiful lady if not by indulging her every whim and childish fantasy? A fantasy that included becoming chatelaine of an English country house.

Pulling up outside the front door Joyti's heart began to race. "Oh wow! All our friends are going to be *soooo* jealous!" Growing up in an inner city slum it was exactly the type of house she'd always dreamed of owning. It said so much about a person — rich, sophisticated; someone with impeccable taste.

The door opened and the estate agent came bouncing out, a beaming smile on his face. Jyoti and Sanjeev climbed out of their Aston Martin.

"Welcome to Wren House. Beautiful property isn't it. And you've chosen the perfect day to view it."

Standing beneath a clear blue sky buffeted by a gentle spring breeze Jyoti couldn't agree more. The smell of sweet violets hung in the air as she took in the Victorian front porch with its freshly painted green door and gleaming brass door knocker.

The agent swept his hand beyond the beautifully manicured gardens and out towards gently sloping fields fringed by woodland. "Gorgeous view. The house comes with the ten acres, give or take… Right, let me show you around."

The estate agent led the way, giving them the guided tour. Every room they went in Jyoti was in complete rapture, gushing about how she would furnish it, the type of colour scheme required, the amazing ambience she would create. Sanjeev listened in silence, nodding his head when required.

An hour or so later and the deal was done. Subject to contract, Wren House was theirs for seven point one million.

But there was a catch.

Sitting in the estate agent's office later that day he explained, "Now this may sound rather odd, and not a little off-putting. Situated within the grounds, though completely out of sight of the main house I might add, is a small cottage..."

"Great." said Sanjeev. "We'll turn it into a granny flat for mum. Just the thing for when she gets ol..."

"Oh no. I'll use it as an office," interrupted Jyoti.

Sanjeev gave her a funny look. "What do you need an office for?"

Conscious of the estate agent staring at her she blurted out, "For my new interior design business!"

This was news to Sanjeev. "I didn't know you were—" Jyoti's foot slammed into his shin. "Oh yes! That's right, you're..."

The agent cut across them, smiling. "Sorry, if you'll just let me explain. This cottage is currently lived in by a couple who..."

Jyoti shot forward in her seat. "A couple? Well they'll just have to leave."

"Absolutely." agreed Sanjeev.

Again the agent gave a diplomatic smile. "It's not that simple, I'm afraid. The current owners will only go ahead with the sale if the buyer agrees to allow the couple to carry on living there."

Jyoti was gobsmacked. "What? I've never heard anything like it! Are they relatives or something?"

"Not as far as I know."

"Then who are they?"

"According to the present owners the couple are no trouble at all. They keep themselves to themselves. You'd hardly know they were there."

"Outrageous!" said Jyoti. "How long have they been living there?"

The agent dug into a file. "Says here they've been tenants of the property now for… Actually it doesn't. Must be a good few years."

The financial side of Sanjeev's brain kicked in. "Tenants? That means they pay rent, right?"

The agent glanced at the file. "Peppercorn rent… Fifty pounds a year."

"What! Fifty pounds a year?" asked Jyoti, gobsmacked. "For a cottage in Cheshire!"

"Written in stone I'm afraid."

"So what you're saying is, even if we buy the house, we can't kick them out or put the rent up?"

"That's correct... Not within the first year, anyhow."

Jyoti drummed her manicured fingers on the desk impatiently. "Explain."

"Well, according to clause thirteen of the contract, once you've lived there for a whole calendar year, you can either renegotiate the rent or terminate the tenancy agreement."

Sanjeev looked at Jyoti hopefully. "That's something at least."

Jyoti shook his head. "A whole year? It's usually a month, isn't it?"

"That's correct," said the agent. "And I have to stress the current owners are particularly insistent upon this."

"Ridiculous. I'm not living next door to a couple of scumbags for a whole year."

The agent gave Jyoti a withering look. "I don't think the current owners would've put up with them if they were scumbags, do you?"

Jyoti sneered.

"Any chance we could have a word with the owners?" asked Sanjeev, trying to calm the situation before his wife exploded. "Maybe they can give us more of an explanation."

"Sorry, I'm afraid that information's confidential."

Jyoti threw her hands up. "Fuck this!" She jumped to her feet. "Come on Sanjeev. Let's get out of here."

Driving back to their house in Hale Barns Jyoti wouldn't let the matter rest. "No way can he be serious, yarr! I mean, who allows a couple of gypsies to live on their property virtually rent-free? The whole situation stinks."

"It's only for a year. Then we can kick them out."

"A lot can happen in a year. We might get murdered in our beds. You hear about things like this all the time."

"What, tenants murdering their landlords? Come off it, darling. Not tenants who are on to a good thing."

Jyoti hated it when Sanjeev was right. She snapped back. "*No!* We'll look for another house."

"OK," said Sanjeev. "There's plenty more on the mark..."

"Oh why do things never work out?! Why are there always problems? Weeks and weeks we've been looking, yarr, and guess what? The one house I like and there's some stupid clause in the contract."

"I can have a word with the agent again if you like?"

"Sanjeev! What good would that do? You heard what he said."

"No harm in..."

"*No!* I'm not having you demeaning yourself. Forget it. Just forget it!"

"Fine."

But Jyoti couldn't forget about it. Over the next few weeks she was hell to live with, complaining about the slightest thing – the cleaner hadn't puddled the curtains properly, the gardener was a lazy good-for-nothing, the neighbours were up themselves.

One evening, arriving home from work, Sanjeev found her sitting in the lounge flicking through a magazine, a tense look on her face. He went to kiss her when she got up and exploded, "I'm sick of living here!"

The reason for her outburst became apparent over dinner. At lunchtime, along with four other women, she'd gone to her friend Bhavna's new house in Prestbury. She obviously didn't like what she saw.

"Oh you should have seen her lording it over us. She took us in every room, even the garage; which she described as 'super heated' whatever *that* means. I had to sit there listening to her drone on about how perfect the house was and how Rajesh had given her an 'unlimited budget' to furnish the place. She kept saying 'unlimited budget' every five minutes. Stupid cow. The woman's nothing but a show-off. I don't know why I bother with her."

"I wouldn't in future, if she's that bad," said Sanjeev.

Jyoti stared out of the window. "If *only* we could have bought Wren House. We'd be *soooo* happy there."

Staring at his wife's miserable face Sanjeev came up with an idea.

The next day he made a few discreet enquiries and found out the names of the couple who were selling Wren House – a Mr. and Mrs. Kenyon. Apparently Mr. Kenyon owned a company called InovaSystems. Sanjeev nearly fell off his chair. It was the same payroll system used by Ahmed Clothing. Sanjeev immediately picked up the phone and rang InovaSystems, asking to speak to Mr. Kenyon. After a short wait he was put through to a Mike Sanders, the CEO. Sanjeev had done his homework; he knew that Mike had started the business nine years ago with Mr. Kenyon. And Mike recognised Sanjeev as heir to his father's global clothing brand, one of InovaSystems biggest customers.

"Oh hi, Mr. Ahmed. We met last year. I don't know if you remember?"

"Yes. You gave my father and I a presentation of your payroll software. We were very impressed. And please, call me Sanjeev."

"What can I do for you, Sanjeev?"

"Is is possible I could speak to you partner, Paul Kenyon?"

"I'm sorry. I'm afraid Paul isn't involved with the business anymore. I bought him out shortly after Christmas. Can I help?"

"Has he started another company, if you don't mind me asking?"

"As a matter of fact he's given up the business altogether." Alarm bells rang in Mike's head. "Are you unhappy with the current software, Sanjeev? If you are we can..."

"No, no. Nothing like that. It's perfect. Perfect... No, what it is, my wife and I are thinking of buying Wren House."

"Oh! Paul's old place," said Mike, relieved. "*Very* nice. I don't live far from there myself."

"Really? I've got a few questions about the house. I was wondering if you had Mr. Kenyon's number? Does he still live in the area?"

"Not anymore. Paul and his wife have gone to live in West Wales. They bought a small holding in... let's see... Llan something or other. All sounds the same to me. I've not spoken to him since I bought him out. Weirdly enough, I rang to wish him happy birthday two days ago and the number came back unobtainable. So I'm afraid I can't help you. Looks like he's done a Jason Bourne."

"I'm sorry?"

"Fallen off the grid."

Sanjeev laughed. "Oh I see... Can I ask you, seeing as you were close friends; why did he sell Wren House?"

Normally Mike wouldn't share personal

information with a stranger but Sanjeev was one of his top clients and who knows, they might end up neighbours. "It might have something to do with his wife, Sarah."

"Oh yes?"

"She took an overdose on Christmas Day. Very sad. Ended up in one of those addiction clinics. I reckon it's got something to do with that... Then again I might be wrong."

"Sorry to hear that. Actually it's to do with the couple who live in a cottage on the property."

"Oh yeah. Those two."

"You've met them?"

"No, no. Paul only mentioned them in passing."

"Sorry to harp on about this, but I'm paying a great deal of money for the house. I just want to know something about them."

"I'm afraid I can't help you. The one time Paul *did* talk about them, which was shortly before he put the house on the market, he said they were two of the nicest people he'd ever met… Let's see now, how did he put it – 'an inspiration.' That's right, he said they were an inspiration. God knows why. They were flat broke by the sound of them."

"Interesting. Thanks for the information, Mike."

"Any time. And do give my regards to your father… Oh, and one last thing, we're currently developing new software that boosts…"

Later that day, while Sanjeev was on his way home from the office he decided to pay another visit to Wren

House. As he drove through the entrance gates he noticed the 'For Sale' sign had been changed to 'Under Offer'. His heart sank. He carried on up the drive. There was the house, bathed in afternoon sunlight. It was even lovelier than before. Sanjeev imagined Jyoti showing her friends round.

They'd be well impressed.

He stopped in front of the house. Climbing out of his Aston Martin he gazed towards the fringe of woodland, behind which, according the estate agent, lay the cottage. Sanjeev knew what to do. He walked through the ornamental garden until he came to a small wooden gate that opened onto a field. He pushed open the gate and strolled through ankle-deep grass. Strange. As he approached the entrance to the woods his heart began to race.

Making his way through the trees he was stunned by the receding carpet of daffodils lining the forest floor. Eventually he caught sight of the cottage. Built of Cheshire brick, with tiny windows and a slate roof topped by a single chimney, it sat serenely in its woodland setting. Surrounding the cottage was a wooden fence enclosing a tiny garden packed with wild flowers. Not that Sanjeev knew their names. Nevertheless the splash of colour took his breath away. As he got closer he noticed half a dozen chickens pecking around the front door. To the right of the cottage was a well-stocked kitchen garden. Sanjeev could see rows and rows of neatly hoed beds ready for planting. Beyond a rickety shed and slanting greenhouse a rough track led further into the woods.

The estate agent was right on both counts; the cottage was well away from the main house, and the tenants were far from scumbags. Standing at the garden gate Sanjeev noticed the cottage was slightly run down — the brickwork needed re-pointing and the front door and the window frames could do with of a lick of paint.

He took a deep breath and walked up the path. Through an open downstairs window came the faint sound of a 1940's crooner backed by the soft tones of a palm court orchestra. He pictured a grey-haired couple in their 80's huddled round a gramophone.

Sanjeev coughed nervously as he tapped on the front door. The muffled sound of a dog barking. Footsteps. The front door creaked open. A tall, slim man dressed in brown corduroy trousers, checked shirt and a Fair Isle tank top stood there smiling. Old fashioned or trendy? It was hard to tell. As was his age. Balding, with a broad friendly face and high forehead, he reminded Sanjeev of one of those soldiers from the First World War who looked forty but were barely eighteen.

"Come in! Come in!" said the man, throwing open the door like he'd know Sanjeev forever. "I'm Jack... Grace! We've got a visitor!"

Printed in Great Britain
by Amazon

19101961R00068